"I'm sincere forgive me.

Mary gazed at him silently. His genuine expression told her he was worth forgiving. "It's okay," she said quietly. "I understood how much pressure you were under, and I felt bad for not being able to assist." She was great at her job, but she couldn't help the vet in surgery.

His brown gaze seemed to take note of her. "You have helped me during these last two days, but in a situation like this, I needed someone with experience."

She nodded. "I'm glad everything worked out in the end."

"Yes," he whispered, as if he was now relieved. "Thank you." His expression softened as he studied her intently. "Will I see you in the morning?"

Mary smiled. "Of course. Where else would I be?"

Dr. Zook grinned, and it did odd things to her insides. "If you wait a minute, I'll walk you out."

Mary nodded and he left to get his coat. She stood there, wondering what she was doing. She couldn't figure out her boss. The last two days had been fine...more than fine, the longer she thought about it.

And that was the problem...

Rebecca Kertz was first introduced to the Amish when her husband took a job with an Amish construction crew. She enjoyed watching the Amish foreman's children at play and swapping recipes with his wife. Rebecca resides in Delaware with her husband and dog. She has a strong faith in God and feels blessed to have family nearby. Besides writing, she enjoys reading, doing crafts and visiting Lancaster County.

Books by Rebecca Kertz

Love Inspired

Loving Her Amish Neighbor
In Love with the Amish Nanny
The Widow's Hidden Past
His Forgotten Amish Love
A Convenient Christmas Wife
Their Fake Amish Betrothal
Her Amish Winter Match

Women of Lancaster County

A Secret Amish Love
Her Amish Christmas Sweetheart
Her Forgiving Amish Heart
Her Amish Christmas Gift

Visit the Author Profile page at LoveInspired.com for more titles.

HER AMISH WINTER MATCH

REBECCA KERTZ

Love Inspired
INSPIRATIONAL ROMANCE

MIX
Paper | Supporting responsible forestry
FSC® C021394

LOVE INSPIRED®
INSPIRATIONAL ROMANCE

ISBN-13: 978-1-335-62132-0

Her Amish Winter Match

Copyright © 2025 by Rebecca Kertz

Love Inspired
22 Adelaide St. West, 41st Floor
Toronto, Ontario M5H 4E3, Canada
www.LoveInspired.com

HarperCollins Publishers
Macken House, 39/40 Mayor Street Upper,
Dublin 1, D01 C9W8, Ireland
www.HarperCollins.com

Printed in Lithuania

Mercy unto you, and peace, and love, be multiplied.
—*Jude* 1:2

For Aunt Jo and Uncle Pat with love

Chapter One

Mary Troyer dreaded coming to work this morning. She had been employed for six months as an assistant to the office manager at Zook Veterinary Clinic, and today would be the first time she'd be alone in the front office since the manager, Beatrice Smithers, had informed staff that she would be out for the foreseeable future. Beatrice's sister Carol had cancer, and there was no one else but Beatrice to care for her. Mary promised she could handle her computer data entry and front desk duties while she was away. The manager had taught Mary the bookkeeping system and other tasks in case the woman was out for a day, but doing both jobs occasionally wasn't the same as doing them indefinitely. The thing she most worried about was dealing directly for the first time with the grumpy owner and only veterinarian in the practice, Dr. Elijah Zook. Who was also her boss.

Mary became more nervous as she neared the clinic and eased her buggy into the clinic's parking lot. She tied her horse to a hitching post with a rope in the barn behind the building, relieved to note that Dr. Zook's car wasn't in the lot yet. She gave her mare water before she left the open structure. After taking the key from her shoulder bag, she pulled a plate of muffins from the back seat. Holding it closely with her left arm, she unlocked the building, walked past the walk-in closet and turned on the lights in the procedure room. It was quiet inside. The silence calmed her and made her feel as if she could handle anything that came at her while Beatrice was away. She put the muffins in the break room down the hall, hoping the treats would ease the stress from Beatrice's absence. She then checked to ensure everything was as it should be in the building. The kennels in the procedure room were clean and waiting for patients. The stainless table, where surgeries were performed, had been disinfected and gleamed under the ceiling lamps. The scent of the cleaning product hung in the air as she looked around the space to see if there was anything left to do.

She went to her desk in the front reception area and turned on the light before she took her cell phone from her bag and booted up her computer. She had plenty of work to do inputting Dr. Zook's handwritten notes on each patient into the electronic medical chart. While the laptop warmed up, she unpacked a new box of dog treats and refilled the jar on the counter, where owners could grab one for their pets. Next, she moved bags of food from the walk-in closet near the rear entrance to shelves in the front behind her desk ready for pickup by clients. When Dr. Zook didn't call or show up by the time she was finished, Mary became apprehensive. He'd never arrived this late. It was nearly seven twenty, and he was usually in by six forty-five at the latest. Had something terrible happened to him? Did he have a car accident? Was he ill?

When fifteen minutes passed with no sign of him, Mary became concerned. She go check the back parking lot. Maybe he was here, taking things out of his car. As she reached out for the knob, the door swung in from the outside. She gasped and pulled up short when Dr. Elijah Zook loomed in the opening. He was at least six inches taller than she. His short, soft sable-brown hair suited him. His bright blue eyes and masculine features would be handsome if he'd quit scowling at her. Like now. The man wore a white shirt, black pants and black sneakers along with his disapproving expression.

"Getting ready to leave already?" he quipped.

"No, I…" She stopped and inhaled sharply to calm herself. "I feared something had happened to you. It's not like you to be late."

He frowned, his gaze traveling down her length as if judging her for her choice of clothing. Mary had donned a tab dress of bright green, simple and appropriately plain, but a nice color for the fall. Over her pinned-back chignon, she wore a white organza prayer *kapp*. The color of her garment had always made her feel uplifted, a feeling she'd need while working with Dr. Zook, who, she knew, would continue to test her during Beatrice's absence. Feeling better about herself was the only way to gain confidence.

She determined to retain her self-assurance as she gazed up at him steadily.

Mary wished he didn't make her so nervous. "I should get back to my desk," she said politely. "Let me know if you need anything. I'm happy to help in any way I can."

The man hmphed, an odd sound that drew her eyes briefly as he moved past her to enter his office.

She unlocked the front door before she returned to her desk. A comment from her mother this morning made it difficult for her to concentrate. *"Dochter, you should be married by now, not working."* She hoped her parents weren't going to pressure her to find a husband. She liked earning money for her family. She loved animals and enjoyed the job. Marriage was the last thing on her mind.

It was close to the arrival of his first patient when Dr. Zook came out to the front desk. He just stood there, staring at her.

"Is something wrong?" she asked. Mary studied him as he opened his mouth and then promptly closed it, as if reluctant to ask her something.

"Do you think you can continue to manage Beatrice's work and yours?" he asked.

"I can handle both," she said and then gave him a reassuring smile.

He blinked, looking surprised but pleased. "I'll pay you extra."

"You will?" she asked, feeling a bit flabbergasted by his offer. "I don't mind doing the work. I find the care you give to your patients fascinating." She grinned. "Although I wouldn't say no to more money." She'd taken the job to help her family, who needed help with finances when they'd moved back after two years away from home. The more she earned the more she could help them. Mary loved animals and enjoyed the job despite Dr. Zook's doubt in her abilities. She was determined to prove to him that she could cover Beatrice's tasks in the office while completing her own work.

Dr. Zook nodded. "Consider it done."

She nodded, too. A glance at the wall clock told her their first patient was five minutes late. "This morning, you have surgeries as well as annual exams, and a problem visit with a female Siberian husky mix who is drinking too much water and having accidents in the house."

He looked concerned. "I'll need to do a litmus test on her first."

Mary frowned, unsure what that was. "What are you thinking?"

"Diabetes." Dr. Zook appeared worried. "But we'll see. If the urine test is positive. I'll have to do a blood test to determine how much insulin she'll need."

"I'm sure you'll figure out how to help her," she said, trying to ease his concern.

He stared at her, as if aggravated with her after her comment, and left, heading toward the back of the building. While he was grouchy more often than not, at least to her, she knew he was a good vet who genuinely cared for animals.

Mary returned to her desk to get to work. It would be worth staying a little later tonight to keep everything the patients' medical charts current, especially with Beatrice gone for the next month at least and most likely longer. And with her new boss watching her so closely, as if waiting for her to make a mistake.

Elijah Zook went into his office and turned on his computer, feeling irritable. While he checked the schedule, he saw that he had a few surgeries this morning. No surprise there—Mary had just said as much. The new office assistant was performing fine but… How was he going to manage without Beatrice? She was truly a wonder. Not only did she schedule patients and keep the books, but before she had hired a new licensed vet tech for him, Beatrice had assisted him with patients in the back. The relatively new vet tech, Diana, performed her job well, too, which had allowed Beatrice to focus on the business side of the office. Mary had been hired to ease Beatrice's load, and he'd seriously questioned Beatrice on her decision to hire the Amish woman, who had little formal training. Beatrice had defended her choice, and he had to admit that Mary worked hard and completed all the tasks assigned to her. Since then, Beatrice had teased him when he was alone for being skeptical of her well-chosen office assistant.

His redheaded vet tech entered the building. "Good morning, Dr. Zook," Diana said with warmth in her green eyes.

Elijah smiled. "Good morning. We have three surgeries this morning. Are you ready for a busy day?"

The young woman nodded. "Sure am. I've got your back," she said. "Just let me hang up my coat."

Her reply made him chuckle as he put on his lab coat while she went into the walk-in closet.

Mary came to the back, her blue eyes somber. "Miss Jackie is here with Bugs," she said, her expression stoic as if she'd recognized early on that she wasn't included in the easy comradery between him and his vet tech.

Bugs was a puppy that was now old enough to be neutered. "Is anyone else in the waiting room?" he asked.

"No," she said, her voice polite, low. "No one is expected until your next surgery at nine thirty."

He eyed her with concern. "Are you all right?"

Her expression softened. "I'm fine."

"Good." Dismissing her, he exited the office and went into the exam room. He saw it had been prepped for surgery, with his operating table disinfected and the smaller stainless steel cart that kept sterilized surgical instruments within his reach.

"I'm ready when you are, Dr. Zook," Diana said, drawing his attention as she entered. Elijah smiled. His assistant was dressed in light blue scrubs with little dogs and cats on them. He knew she owned several sets of scrubs, each one featuring different animals. In startling contrast, Mary wore an Amish tab dress in green with her blond hair pinned up and covered with a white prayer *kapp*. The only thing that was different in her appearance from day to day was the color she wore. Her garments were as familiar to him as those of the women from his painful childhood, except in his community the women had worn dark dresses and black kerchiefs as head coverings.

Diana held Bugs, a blond male corgi retriever with a pink-

and-black nose. "Mary told Miss Jackie to go home and some-one will call her when Bugs is ready to leave."

"Your idea or hers?" He pulled out packaged instruments and set them on the mobile table.

Diana eyed him curiously. "Hers. It's standard procedure, isn't it?"

"It is. I'm glad she knows it," he said with approval. Diana placed the dog on the operating table, unclipped his leash, then stroked his thick fluffy fur as she held him in place while he prepared the anesthesia for the procedure. He had always loved animals, and becoming a vet had seemed like the ideal career path for him. But he'd never expected it to include dealing with stress brought on by staff changes. Elijah wanted people he could trust to be there when he needed them. Beatrice's absence upset him and he feared he'd taken his frustration out on Mary, who was working while his office manager was not. The realization made him feel ashamed.

"So, Bugs's blood work was good?" Diana asked.

"It was fine." Elijah was glad, as it meant he could safely anesthetize Bugs.

The surgery went quickly, and soon Elijah's patient was moved into a kennel so they could watch him until Eli was satisfied that Bugs could go safely home.

Mary popped her head through the open doorway as he and Diana cleaned up and prepared for the next patient. "Miss Jackie is on the phone. She wants to know how Bugs is doing. Do you want to talk with her? Or should I?"

"I'll be happy to talk with her," Elijah said. He gave her a small smile to convince her that he approved of her ques-tion, that he preferred to talk with owners if time allowed. Mary nodded and turned to leave. "Mary? Remind me when our next appointment is." As he spoke, he noticed how she had gazed at Bugs, as if she wanted to approach and pet him through the kennel bars.

Mary blinked, then met his gaze. "Nine thirty, so you have a short break before then. Did either of you eat breakfast?"

He shrugged. "Wasn't hungry."

"I ate," Diana said.

"I brought muffins. I've left them in the break room," Mary said, capturing his attention. Then she quickly left the room.

After he spoke with Miss Jackie, assuring her Bugs was doing well, Elijah entered the break room where a sink, a refrigerator, a microwave, along with a coffeepot and a table with four chairs were situated. He poured himself a cup of coffee, then sat down. He could use a pick-me-up, and he was surprised by Mary's thoughtfulness in bringing food. He knew better than to go without eating, but he'd been late getting up and had rushed to get to the office to start his day on time.

The Amish woman came into the room moments later, uncovered a plate and set it in the middle of the table. "I made these last night—chocolate chip and blueberry. They're still fresh."

He studied her as she uncovered the dish. Then she turned to leave. "Mary," he called. She halted and faced him. "Thank you for breakfast."

She beamed at him, and Elijah could only stare. When she smiled, he recognized her beauty that he'd seemed unable to see until that moment. The fact that he saw it now bothered him.

"Anytime," she murmured. "I'll let you know when your next patient checks in." Then she walked out of the room, leaving him alone.

Elijah frowned, impressed but trying not to be. He didn't need to see her as an attractive woman or see her as anyone other than an employee. Plus, her clothing was a daily reminder of the faith he'd once been part of…and a past that was full of painful memories for his entire family.

"Tea!" Diana exclaimed when she entered the room and made herself a cup of tea with a teabag that Mary must have left for her. "Everything is ready for patient number two."

"Good." He gestured toward the muffin plate. "Are you sure you're not hungry enough for one of those?"

"Maybe." Diane grinned and grabbed one before she took the chair across from him.

Mary returned a few minutes later. "Princess is here. I just checked her in. Her owner, Mrs. Mason, is early and is prepared to wait until you're ready, so feel free to take your time." She frowned and then bit her lip. "If you want, that is."

Elijah studied her, realizing then that his behavior had made her uncomfortable. "Diana will be out as soon as we're done."

"Thanks for the tea," Diana said as she held up her cup. "A citrus blend?"

Mary nodded, with a slight smile that vanished when she met his gaze. As he watched her go, Elijah frowned, disturbed by the sudden realization that she intrigued him.

Chapter Two

Late that afternoon, Elijah cleaned and prepped the procedure room for the next day. The front office had run smoothly today, despite everything they had to accomplish. Mary had done better than he'd expected in handling her and Beatrice's workload in Beatrice's absence. Earlier in the day, he'd caught a glimpse of her working. He stood a moment, impressed with how meticulously she'd entered the data from his messy, handwritten medical charts into the system. Then she'd seen him and frowned, asking if there was something she could do for him. And when he'd approached the waiting room after lunch to assure a pet owner that his cat was fine, he noticed how kind and compassionate she'd been as she'd interacted with his patients' owners.

Mary was unlike any Amish women he'd known in the past, who only ever attended to the house, not worked away from home. She was always ready to roll up her sleeves and do whatever was asked of her in the office. He certainly couldn't fault her work ethic.

"I'm going to head home," Diana said, interrupting his thoughts, as she came into the room with her coat over her arm. "Unless you need me for anything else."

Elijah smiled. "Go on. Thanks for your help today."

"We got a lot done," she said as she put on her coat. "Have a nice evening."

"The same to you," he told her before she left through the rear door, which left only Mary still in the office.

He pulled up the next day's schedule in his office and noted that it would be filled with annual and problem exams but no surgeries. As he took off his lab coat and hung it on a wall hook, his thoughts returned to Mary. She'd told him that members of her Amish community were allowed to use computers in places of business. Many Amish store owners used them to keep track of their inventory as well as sales. The church elders first had permitted cell phones in case of emergencies or calling out of work sick but later decided that phones could used for more. Which surprised him.

The Amish community he'd belonged to as a boy had forbidden all technology, including the use of cell phones. His community also would have frowned upon working in an Englisher office. Surely there were other places, Amish-owned businesses, that would have hired her. He couldn't help wondering why she'd applied here of all places.

Before he could decide whether it was wise or not, Elijah impulsively went to the front office to find out. "May I ask you something?" he said as she met his gaze and stood. When she nodded, he continued, "Why do you want to work here? What made you apply for the job?"

She bit her lip as she hesitated. "My family needs the money, and no one else pays as well as you do."

He frowned, more curious than he'd been when he entered. "I know I shouldn't ask this, but why does your family need money?"

"Does it matter?" As if embarrassed, Mary averted her gaze as she shifted file folders around on her desk.

"You don't have to tell me," he assured her, suddenly feeling regretful about how he'd handled things. "I just wondered. Your reasons are your own."

She met his gaze directly then. "You want to know?"

Elijah nodded.

Her expression became solemn. "My family left our house in New Berne for over two years after an emergency visit to New Wilmington because my grandfather was ill and not expected to live." Sadness entered her blue eyes, making them glisten. "He didn't die, and we are grateful and feel blessed, but then something happened to keep us there." She paused as if it was too painful for her to go on.

"It's not my business," he said softly. He instantly felt bad for asking, as he realized how rude he must have sounded, how nosy. "You don't have to tell me."

Mary gave him a small smile. "It's okay. It was my older brother. He had an accident and ended up in the hospital."

"I'm sorry," Elijah whispered, studying her as compassion welled up inside him. Life hadn't been easy for her and her family either, he realized. "That must have been rough."

Blue eyes glistening, Mary nodded. She shut down her computer, then faced him, appearing suddenly uncomfortable with how much of her family business she'd confessed to him. "If you don't need me to do anything else, I'm going to head home. I'll be in early tomorrow to catch up on the patient charts."

"You don't have to do that," he said with concern.

"I'd like to. I don't mind at all." She studied him as if trying to read his thoughts. "Unless you'd rather I not."

He shrugged. "It's up to you." Elijah watched her put on her coat. "I'll walk you out." He opened the door for her, and she preceded him in silence. After closing the door behind him, he watched her enter the barn, lead her horse out by a rope and climb into her buggy. He waited for her to leave the parking lot before he put on his coat, locked the building and drove home.

Once inside his small house, he grabbed cold pizza from his refrigerator. Then he sat in a chair by the window with his food untouched on a tray table and stared at the large oak tree in his backyard. A cardinal flew past and disappeared among the leaves. A reminder that life went on, no matter how hard it could be at times.

He took a bite of the leftover pizza and sipped from his can of cola, focusing on his supper in an attempt to force Mary from his thoughts. Listening to her speak of her family's trials reminded him what had happened to his family when he was ten years old. How could he ever forget what his former Amish community had done to them after his family was shunned and banished by their strict and conservative church elders over a misunderstanding?

Young Elijah couldn't believe his family had been judged so harshly. He had tried to talk to the church elders after, get them to see his family's side of things, but they'd refused to listen. They had shunned his family and acted as if Elijah wasn't there.

Which was why he hadn't liked or trusted the Amish faith since. Judgmental and unforgiving, the church elders in his former community had made life difficult for him, his brothers and his parents. Life had taken a dark turn where they'd struggled emotionally and financially after leaving the only way of life they'd ever known. It had been years before a hint of light shone at the end of the tunnel.

Mary was different from the other Amish women from his childhood in more ways than one. She worked hard to give her family the money they needed, and he respected that. And hadn't he done the same thing? Tried to financially help his parents once he was old enough at sixteen to work part-time?

He sighed and took another bite of pizza, exhausted from the long workday—the first of many without his trusted office manager. But Beatrice knew what she was doing when she hired Mary, and he shouldn't have had any concerns. He just hoped they could make it through the next month at the clinic without her.

Mary woke up Tuesday morning before dawn and was able to get her chores at home done before she headed into work early. Since the clinic wouldn't open until seven thirty today, there would be plenty of time for her to catch up on her computer work. She debated whether to drive in at this time since it was dark when she left the house and dark in the afternoon when she left the office. But her work ethic wouldn't allow her to stay home later when she could use the extra hours to catch up.

This morning, she'd brought the homemade doughnuts she'd baked the night before. The food she'd brought into the office had been well received so she decided she'd bring in more to share whenever she could. It might help ease stress while Beatrice was away. Before Diana and Dr. Zook came in, she'd make a pot of coffee.

Yesterday had gone much better than she'd anticipated. She'd been able to handle most everything in the office just as Beatrice wanted. At her desk, Mary booted up her computer and then pulled out the stack of remaining handwritten medical charts, which needed to be entered into a data system that listed patients, their owners' names and the animals' history with Zook Veterinary Clinic. She left the bag of doughnuts on the break room counter and turned on the coffeepot before she returned to her desk. She then checked the schedule so that she knew what patients to expect that day.

Fifteen minutes later, the front door opened, and their first client entered the waiting room with her pet.

"Good morning," Mary greeted the woman. "Who do

we have here today?" She leaned over the counter to see an adorable Yorkshire terrier. "Is this Junior here for his annual physical?"

The woman smiled. "Yes, he is."

"Wonderful, Mrs. Johnson." Mary beamed at her. "Why don't you take a seat, and someone will bring you into an exam room shortly." She let Dr. Zook know who was here, and Diana came out to get owner and patient a few moments later.

The day went well. Mary was able to keep up as receptionist and still work on the books. After the last patient had left, she locked the door, then went to see if there was anything she could do to help Dr. Zook and Diana.

"I'm almost done, but thanks for asking," Diana said as she disinfected the instrument table.

With a nod, Mary returned to her desk to input the data from today's medical notes into her computer. She heard Diana call out that she was leaving and would see her tomorrow.

A half hour later, she was getting ready to turn off her computer when a heavy pounding on the practice's front door startled her. Mary went into the waiting room and peeked through the window. A young redheaded woman stood outside the clinic entrance, her arms holding a wrapped bundle. Mary hurried to open the door.

"Oh!" the woman cried. "Please, can you help this kitten?" She held up the little creature squirming in a towel. "It ran in front of my car, and I couldn't stop in time."

"Stay here," Mary said after a glimpse at the kitten's face. She ran back to Dr. Zook's office where he was working. "Dr. Zook. We have an emergency. You have a new patient that needs your help. A woman brought in a cat she hit with her car."

He pushed back his seat and hurried to the waiting room.

Mary followed, watching as he soothed the distressed woman and carefully extracted the wounded cat from her arms. The kitten had a striped coat of orange and tan with pretty amber eyes and a cute nose. She was surprised to see that it didn't have a long tail but one that looked as if it had been cut off. Someone, she was sure, must be frantically searching for this beautiful young cat.

"What's your name?" Dr. Zook asked the woman.

"Bridget," she said brokenly.

"Bridget, can you tell me where you hit him?" he asked, his voice gentle. "Full-on? Or did you just graze him as he ran across the road?"

"I think I just grazed the back of him," she said, hugging herself with her arms.

Dr. Zook nodded. "Thank you. I'll take care of him." He then disappeared into the back.

"He's in good hands," Mary assured Bridget. "The exam and evaluation may take a while. You may have a seat or go home."

"I'd rather wait here for some news," the redhead said with tears in her brown eyes.

Mary nodded, then with heart racing, she hurried toward the back to see if there was anything she could do to help with the wounded animal since Diana had already left. Understanding how the woman felt, she sent up a silent prayer for the kitten to be all right.

She hesitated before she entered the procedure room. "Dr. Zook?"

He didn't look up from his patient.

Chapter Three

Mary studied Elijah in his white lab coat bending over the injured kitten on a stainless steel table as she approached. His hands were gentle as he ran his fingers over the animal's flanks. "Dr. Zook?" she called again.

"Yes?" The look in his eyes gave her pause.

"I thought I could help you," she ventured carefully, hoping not to irritate him.

"You're not a certified vet tech," he explained, his gaze focused on his patient. "I'll have to handle this on my own."

"Is there anything you need?" she asked.

He shot her another look. "Can't you see I'm busy and can't be disturbed?"

Mary felt inadequate as she left the room and returned to her desk. She sat, staring into space for a moment before common sense took over, and she began to worry that maybe Dr. Zook was right. She picked up the phone and tried to reach Diana, but the young woman didn't answer. She frowned, debating what to do.

The young woman who had hit the animal got up from her chair in the waiting room and approached. "Any word on his injuries?" Bridget said with concern in her expression.

"Not yet, but I'll see if I can find out," Mary replied. She went to the back room. "Dr. Zook? Is there anything I can tell Bridget about your patient's injuries?"

"No, I'm still assessing him." He shot her an angry glance. "I'll be out once I know. So, do me a favor and let me work!"

Hurt, Mary went back to the front desk. "Bridget, Dr. Zook is still examining him and as soon as he knows more, he'll give you an update."

"Thank you," the woman said with tears in her eyes.

Mary nodded. "Can I get you a cup of coffee or tea while you wait?"

"No thank you," she replied. "I'm too upset to drink anything."

"I understand." Mary returned to the back room. She knew her boss felt stressed because this was an emergency and Diana wasn't here to help him. "What if I reassure him while you examine him? I can pet him and calm him with my voice. Am I allowed to do that?"

Dr. Zook looked up and met her gaze. She waited nervously as he studied her. The kitten gave a pitiful meow. He sighed before he nodded. "Fine. That may help. Come and stand over here." He gestured toward the other side of the table near the cat's head, where she could get close enough to do what needed to be done.

Eager to help, Mary followed his lead and then began to stroke him where he wasn't injured, murmuring to him as she watched Dr. Zook work. She noted how gentle Dr. Zook's hands were as he examined his patient thoroughly.

"I'm going to take an X-ray," he said softly. "I'd appreciate it if you'd continue to soothe him so he remains still and we can get good images."

Mary nodded and followed Dr. Zook's directions, carefully moving the kitten to the X-ray machine.

"Here, put these on for protection," Elijah instructed as he handed her a shield and gloves, which she quickly donned.

She was amazed at how gentle he was with the animal.

The kitten no longer seemed as frightened as he was when he'd first arrived. She murmured soothingly and rubbed the patient's head and neck while Dr. Zook x-rayed the injured back leg and surrounding area. Then he did an ultrasound of his entire rear body.

When he was done, the man turned a smile in Mary's direction. Her heart started to race and she experienced a funny feeling in her stomach. "He'll be fine," he said after he'd cleaned and bandaged the small wound. "Thankfully he has no broken bones."

Mary grinned. "I'm glad. I know Bridget is worried about him." When Dr. Zook bent to pick up his patient, she hurried to a kennel and opened the door for him. He moved carefully, soothing him with low murmurs as he placed the kitten into the clean kennel. "May I ask you a question?" When he nodded, she said, "Why does the cat barely have a tail?"

He grinned. "He's an American Bobtail. Their bobbed tail is part of the breed."

"Oh." Mary blushed, affected by his good humor. "Will you talk with Bridget? She's extremely upset."

Dr. Zook closed and latched the kennel door, then met her gaze. "Tell her I'll be right out."

Feeling good about what they'd done, Mary returned to the front desk. "Dr. Zook will be out soon to let you know how his patient is."

Bridget blinked back tears as she gazed at her across the room. "Thank you."

Mary smiled. "He's a good man who cares about the animals."

A few moments later, Dr. Zook walked past the front desk and entered the waiting room. Bridget stood up, looking concerned.

"The little guy will be fine," he said. "I've done an X-ray

and ultrasound. There is no damage to his internal organs. He has a cut on his right hind leg." He met the woman's gaze. "I've cleaned and dressed it. Don't you worry about him. I did a microchip scan and found his owner. I'm going to keep him here until she comes to pick him up."

"I want to pay his bill," Bridget said. "And I need to tell his owner that I'm sorry for not being able to avoid hitting him."

"You must have steered away from him as soon as you realized he was in the road," he said. "Your quick reflexes assured that he wasn't hurt worse."

Mary saw a different man when he smiled.

"This is all good news, Bridget," Elijah continued. "Go home and get some rest. I already told Mrs. Rhodes what happened. She's coming to get him and is pleased that he's been found relatively unharmed."

"Thank you," Bridget gushed. "I'll be forever grateful." She reached for her purse on the chair behind her. "I have my credit card—"

"Payment can wait until tomorrow morning," Dr. Zook said.

Bridget nodded, thanked him again and left through the front door. Mary watched him lock up, then picked up her purse and headed toward the back to leave.

"Mary, stop please," Dr. Zook called. She turned to see him coming toward her.

"I… I wanted to apologize for my earlier bad behavior." He appeared genuinely regretful. "I was worried about my patient and the fact that Diana was unavailable to assist." The man offered a small smile. "Thanks for soothing him while I did what I had to do." He released a sharp breath. "I'm sincerely sorry for snapping at you, and I hope you'll forgive me."

Mary gazed at him silently, noting his expression that told her he was worth forgiving. "It's okay," she said quietly. "I understood how much pressure you were under, and I felt bad for not being able to do more to help."

His blue gaze seemed to take note of her. "You've done a good job these last two days, but in this situation, I needed someone with experience. But calming him made it easier for me, and I'm grateful you were there. You were wonderful with him."

She smiled, relieved. "I'm glad everything worked out in the end."

"Yes," he whispered as if he had been concerned but was now relieved. "Thank you." His expression was soft as he studied her intently. "Will I see you in the morning?"

Mary grinned. "Of course. Where else would I be?"

Dr. Zook's smile did odd things to her insides. "If you wait a minute, I'll walk you out. I'll be staying awhile to keep an eye on Fluffball until his owner picks him up. She promised to be here before seven."

"Fluffball?" she said, amused.

"That's what Mrs. Rhodes said his name was after I called her to tell her what happened."

After agreeing to wait a moment, Mary grabbed her cape, wondering what she was doing. She couldn't figure out her boss and employer. The last two days had been fine…more than fine, the longer she thought about it. Until the emergency happened, and then she felt as if she'd wanted to melt into nothing or slip out the door to avoid the stress of Dr. Zook's bad humor.

He was back in less than a minute without his lab coat but with his car keys in one hand and a doughnut from the break room in the other. After slipping his keys into his pants pocket, he opened the door for her. "Do you want this last one?" he asked, holding out the treat toward her.

She laughed. "You eat it. I have more of those at home."

"Thanks for bringing them today." He walked her to the door and led her outside.

"I'll bring something else for breakfast tomorrow if you're interested," she said as he started to walk with her toward her buggy.

"I'm interested." She felt him watching her as she untied her horse and climbed into her buggy.

"Wait," he called. "Thank you again for your help."

She smiled as she picked up the leathers. "You're most welcome."

He stepped back from her vehicle.

"Have a good night, Dr. Zook."

"You, too, Mary. See you first thing in the morning," he replied, his blue eyes warmer than she'd seen them before.

Mary didn't wait for him to return inside. She drove from the lot, her thoughts whirling with thoughts of her boss.

Elijah waited for Mary to leave before he went back into the clinic. He was glad that Fluffball's injuries weren't severe. He felt bad for snapping at Mary earlier; she was only trying to help. Her offer to keep the kitten calm was a good one. She'd done a wonderful job as she petted and murmured assurances to him.

He checked on his charge again, pleased to see him resting comfortably. He filled his mug with coffee and went to get work done in his office. He handwrote his medical notes on Fluffball. He never liked working on a computer, although he knew they helped to run his practice. His love-hate relationship with technology had been carried over from his family's time in their Nebraska Amish community in Mifflin County, eighty-three miles northwest of Lancaster. Eventually, he got used to using it after learning how in school. He often checked his schedule on the computer and looked up medical records after Mary had added them to his patient electronic charts.

He stared at his cell phone on his desk. When he first bought it, he'd almost tossed it. The phone had reminded him of the pain his family had suffered when they'd been shunned. His brother Aaron had found a cell phone in the road near the general store and waited to see if someone would come back for it. When no one claimed it, he'd immediately brought it to his parents to give to the church elders. But the elders had learned of the phone from someone within the community, who'd seen Aaron walking down the street with it. Within minutes of Aaron's return home, two of the elders had shown up on the Zooks' doorstep. The elders' sour faces as they asked his mother and father to step outside should have been a clue that something was seriously wrong. One elder, a preacher, demanded that his father hand over the cell phone, and his mother went inside to get it. After it was handed over, his father tried to explain, but the elders stopped him. They informed them that they were no longer welcome in the community. Elijah's family was shunned because technology was sinful, and they were guilty of possessing it. The men had turned away from them, leaving his parents shocked. They had always been good and faithful members of the Nebraska Amish.

Elijah had rebelled against owning a phone for years after his family left. But then he realized it made more sense to have one in case there was a family or an animal emergency.

He flipped through the files he'd pulled earlier. He thought of his brother Jacob, an equine vet in a large veterinary practice, the New Berne Animal Hospital, a half hour away from his place by car. Yet, despite working in the same field, the only time they saw each other was when the family ate together at his parents' house.

Elijah glanced at his wall clock and realized that he'd been thinking and not working for nearly an hour. He closed the file folder before him and shifted it to the pile on the left side of his desk. Then he went into the back to check on his patient, hoping that Fluffball was awake. Elijah examined him quickly again, offered him food and took him carefully to the litterbox he kept for his feline patients. Then he returned the kitten to the kennel and waited for his owner.

The doorbell at the rear entrance at this late hour surprised him. He was expecting Mrs. Rhodes to knock at the front door or call when she arrived. He answered it, stunned to find Mary standing in the dark with a foil-covered plate in her hands.

"Has Mrs. Rhodes been by to pick up Fluffball?" she asked.

"Not yet." He eyed her with curiosity. "What are you doing back here?" he asked gently.

Mary appeared uncertain. "I thought you might like some supper."

Elijah gazed at her a long moment. "That's thoughtful of you." He opened the door wider and stepped back. "Come in."

"I can't stay. My *mam* is expecting me." She held out the plate. "It's roast beef with mashed potatoes and green beans. I hope you like them."

He accepted her offering. "Yum," he said, unable to help his grin. He was warmed by how thoughtful she was. "Thank you. I appreciate it. I decided I'd have to wait until I could get home and make something. Now I don't have to." He saw her shiver, although she was wearing a dark woolen cloak. "Are you all right to drive home? If you wait a bit, I'll be able to take you and return to pick you up in the morning. You can leave your horse and buggy in the barn." The insulation in the barn was good protection against the cold.

Her eyes turned warm. "Thank you, Dr. Zook, but I'll be fine. My younger brother, Simeon, is with me."

Elijah saw a young man seated in the driver's seat of the buggy under the streetlight. "I'm glad you didn't come alone." The scent of the meat rose to tantalize his nose. He gestured with the plate. "It smells delicious."

She smiled and nodded. "Fluffball still doing okay?"

"As well as expected," he said. "He'll be fine."

Cold air filtered into the room, and Mary seemed to realize it. "I should go. I'll see you in the morning, Dr. Zook."

"Be safe heading home," he said. Although he felt the cold November breeze, he watched as she climbed into the buggy before her brother drove them away.

Leaving the back room lights on, he shut and locked the door, then brought his supper into the break room. Elijah was surprised by the full meal. Some Amish families ate their large meals at lunchtime. Mary's family must like eating a big meal in the evening. At least, today they did, he thought with a smile.

He grabbed a bottle of water from the fridge and a fork from a drawer, then sat down to enjoy his meal. It was every bit as delicious as it smelled. There was plenty of food, and he felt filled up when he was done. Then, after washing the dish, he went to check on his patient and gave him a few pets. Next, he brought his water into the office and set it on his desk.

He heard the bell at the front door alerting him that Mrs. Rhodes was here for Fluffball. He went to let her in.

"Mrs. Rhodes?" he asked.

"Yes, it's me." She looked to be in her sixties. "How is he?"

"He's doing well." He waved toward the hallway. "Have a seat and I'll bring him to you."

Elijah brought her the kitten and Mrs. Rhodes exclaimed over the sight of him. "He'll be fine," he assured her. "Bridget, the woman who brought him in, was worried sick about him. She wants to pay his bill. She did everything she could to avoid him with her car."

"She doesn't have to pay for him," she said. "I'm happy to take care of the bill. How much was his care?" After he named a figure for the kitten's care, the woman wrote out a check and handed it to him. "Thank you, Dr. Zook. Please tell—Bridget, is it?" He nodded, and she continued. "Tell her I appreciate all she has done for him, bringing him here to you. I'm grateful to have him back. Better yet, may I call her to thank her?"

"I'll check with her when I hear from her tomorrow and let you know her number if she agrees." He then saw her and Fluffball out through the front door before closing and re-locking it.

Once she'd left, Elijah sighed with relief as he shut everything down for the night. He drove home, eager to unwind and relax. He was ready to make an early night of it and go straight to bed, drifting off to sleep easily. Until in the middle of the night, he was jerked awake by a nightmare. He sprang upright and breathed deeply.

It wasn't the first time he'd had the dream, yet it continued to occasionally haunt him. He'd dreamt of the time after the shunning. His painful past had made him bitter, and he'd found it hard to let the bitterness go.

His family had suffered and been forced to move from their home. Ripped from their community, life had become difficult for his family, especially his parents, who'd struggled emotionally and financially. They'd been poor for years after leaving Mifflin County, having to relocate to Lancaster County, where they saw Amish living their lives here peacefully yet were unable to join them because of the shunning. As soon as he, Jacob and Aaron were old enough, they'd found part-time jobs after school to help with their money situation and then full-time jobs during the summer. As the youngest, Elijah had wanted to quit school and work full-time the same as his brothers did, but his parents had insisted he continue his education like Aaron and Jacob had. The money his parents had received from the sale of their old property hadn't lasted long. His mother had earned money from sewing clothes and doing alterations from Englishers. His father had set up shop in the garage of the small house they'd rented and worked to earn a living making furniture like he used to in Big Valley.

Englishers, Elijah thought with a scowl. They had become Englishers themselves through no desire of their own. Although he'd moved past the pain of his former life for the most part, there were times when nightmares of the shunning haunted his sleep, bringing everything that had changed for him and his family that day.

Chapter Four

"*Dochter*, when are you going to invite Dr. Zook to join us for supper?" Mam asked before Mary drove to the clinic the next morning. "You've worked for the man for how many months now? Five?"

"Six months," Mary replied, surprised by her mother's request.

Her *mam* clicked her tongue. "And we haven't met him yet."

Mary shook her head. "He's my boss, not my beau." At times, he was friendly, and during others, he seemed to barely tolerate her.

"Does it matter?" her mother said. "You spend more time with him than you do our family."

"It's my job. I work more hours now because Beatrice is out for a while." She put on her black woolen cape, ready to head into work. "Last night when I handed the meal to him, Dr. Zook looked happy to get your roast beef and sides."

Her mother's lips curved upward. "At least I know he is a commonsense man who enjoys good cooking."

Simeon entered through the side door and hung up his jacket. "I readied the buggy for you, Mary. Be careful, it's dark and cold outside this time of morning."

"Thanks." Mary reached for her black bonnet and put it on over her white *kapp*. She then grabbed a black scarf, winding it around her neck. She'd been glad when her brother had driven her back to the clinic to deliver food to her boss. "Simeon," she said. "I appreciate your taking me to the clinic last night."

He rubbed his arms with his hands as if to warm them. "I couldn't let you drive back to the clinic alone. It's not safe." He reached out and swiped a piece of bread from the cutting board on the counter where their mother had sliced a full loaf for breakfast. "I don't know how you can stand going in so early every day."

"I heard that, and Simeon is right," her father said as he came into the room. "It's dangerous to be out and about in the hours before the sun rises in the morning and after it sets. You should ask Dr. Zook if he'll allow you to change your workday to daylight hours."

"Dat, I can't do that," Mary said as worry rose in to almost choke her. "It's a *gut* job, and I'm trying my best to make sure I get all my work done. It won't be for much longer, just until Beatrice returns." Being up early every day messed with her ability to think clearly until she'd had a few cups of coffee.

"Would you like me to speak with him?" her father offered.

"*Nay!*" Mary exclaimed. "Please don't do that. I'll talk with him and see what he has to say, but know that while Beatrice is out, I'm working to handle her job as well as my own." She bit her lip and then remembered Elijah's offer. "He said he'd pay me extra because of it."

"You don't need to work at all, as far as I'm concerned," Dat said.

"Dat, you know I do." Mary helped her mother put out the food before taking her usual seat across from Simeon. Her parents made a habit of sitting at each end when it was just the four of them at the table.

"I don't like you seeing you work this hard, *dochter*."

Samuel Troyer took his seat. "You do more than you should. You're not getting any younger, Mary. It's time you think of marrying and having a family."

"Dat, there is plenty of time for that," Mary said. "I work because I enjoy the job. I have plenty of time to settle down."

Her father frowned. "Mary…"

"Please, *Vadder*," she pleaded, interrupting him. "I'll ask to change my hours. *Okey?* Please don't make me quit. I enjoy seeing all the animals, checking them in. And besides I'm almost caught up with Beatrice's work so I won't have to stay as long." She put her phone into her purse. "I need to go. I'll see you later."

Her *mam* smiled. "Mary, I still think the man should come to a meal so we can take the man's measure."

"*Mudder*, he's my employer and nothing more," she reiterated, with a growing feeling of horror. "Please. The job pays well, and as I already told you, Dr. Zook promised me an increase in wages. This is a *gut* thing."

"Hmm," Dat said as he sat back in his chair. Her father had a touch of gray in his brown hair and beard with blue eyes that both of her brothers had inherited, as well as the way he smiled. Mary had inherited his eye color but unlike her dark-haired brothers, she had blond hair.

"What does that 'hmm' mean, Dat?" Simeon said, clearly curious and amused by his sister's conversation with their parents.

Her father studied Mary thoughtfully. "It means I'll need to think on this for a while—"

"Think about what?" Mary replied quickly, worried about their interference in her work life. She and Elijah Zook were getting along a little better now. The last thing she needed was for them to embarrass her.

Her father chuckled. "Nothing for you to worry about, *dochter.*"

"That's what you think," she murmured beneath her breath. "What makes you believe there is anything you should do when everything is already going well for me at the office?" All she needed to do was prove to her employer that she was more than capable of handling all the work expected of her, while keeping her parents happy and at bay. It was important to her to prove to Elijah and Beatrice that she could do the extra work.

If her father interfered, then things would worsen. Mary sent up a silent prayer that her parents respected her desire to let her deal with Elijah Zook on her own. She knew they loved her, but she was old enough to handle herself whenever needed. "I'll talk with him tomorrow," she said, trying to gauge her father's reactions. "See if I can come in later and leave earlier than I have been." If she had to work through lunch to get things done, she'd do it. When her father didn't respond, Mary became nervous.

Nonetheless, she went in for her next shift as usual. When she arrived at work, Mary saw Dr. Zook's car in the lot. After she hung up her cloak, she headed to take a quick peek inside Elijah's office and caught a glimpse of him on his cell phone. His brow furrowed, and her employer didn't look happy about the conversation, so she went to her workstation, turned on her computer and then went to place the sausage, egg and cheese casserole she'd brought into the break room refrigerator. Once back at her desk, she went over the day's schedule. Moments later, Dr. Zook entered the reception area. She looked up and frowned at his worried expression.

"What's wrong?" she asked.

"Diana called in sick. It's just you and me today." He scowled with displeasure. "We can only do the best we can."

Mary nodded. "Please let me know whatever I can do to help." She studied the electronic calendar again. "Your schedule isn't bad. You have four patient exams and two appointments for dog grooming. Diana usually does those, doesn't she?"

Dr. Zook nodded, appearing thoughtful. "She does. I can manage the annuals. I recognize the patients on the schedule. The dogs who will be in later for grooming mostly need to be bathed." He met and held her gaze, his blue eyes serious. "Can you help me with those?"

She was pleased that he'd asked, yet she felt her heart rate spike at the thought of doing something wrong while helping. "If you tell or show me what to do."

His lips curving a little, he nodded. "Fair enough."

Mary relaxed. The man's small, rare smile caused a fluttering in her stomach.

"Fluffball's owner picked him up last evening as arranged, and she paid the bill," he said. "She was happy to have him home and pleased at how well he was doing. Let me know when my first patient arrives, please. Until then, I'll get some work done in my office."

"Will do." As he started to leave, she said, "Dr. Zook, did you have breakfast?"

He stopped and faced her. "I did. Thanks for asking." He held her gaze for a few seconds, and the impact of his blue gaze made her cheeks warm. "And please call me Elijah during off-hours."

"Elijah." Mary smiled. "I brought a breakfast casserole," she told him, "We can eat it later for lunch if you want."

He took a couple steps closer, making her overly aware of his good looks. "Sausage or bacon?" he asked.

Mary couldn't keep her eyes off him. "Sausage, egg and cheese."

"Sounds good." He started to walk out again.

"Elijah?" she said, stopping him. "Have you had breakfast casserole before?"

"My mother used to make it," he replied. "A friend taught her how."

"An Amish friend?" She couldn't help wondering.

He shrugged, but she saw his mouth firm before it softened. "She didn't say who taught her."

"If you ever want good food, you should try Fannie's Luncheonette over on Main St. They are open for breakfast and lunch. The casserole came from there." Mary didn't mention that Fannie was her sister-in-law.

"I may do that after I taste it." A teasing glimmer entered his blue eyes, and Elijah smiled. He seemed to assess her as if seeing her anew. "Thank you." Then he left the room.

Mary enjoyed bringing food to share. It was just the way things worked in her community. She and her family were always willing to share whatever they had with others, just as visitors were welcomed into their home.

Mary recalled how his expression had darkened briefly after she'd asked who had taught his mother how to make breakfast casserole. He seemed to relax once she'd suggested he eat at Fannie's Luncheonette. Elijah Zook was a complex man, and she couldn't figure out why. There were so many facets to him that she didn't understand. Although, it unsettled her a little to realize that she wanted to.

Elijah came up to the front desk the next morning. "Diana quit," he told her, clearly upset. "She's eloping with her fiancé who's in the Air Force, so she's going with him to his next assignment."

Mary was shocked to hear the news about her coworker. She thought that she and Diana had become friends; yet, the tech had left without even saying goodbye to her. "So, it's just the two of us now," she said, trying to hide how hurt she felt.

"Yes, until we can hire another vet tech." Much to her surprise, he pulled out the chair beside her and sat down.

"Want coffee?" she asked as she stood. "Our first appointment isn't for another hour and we can talk about what to do next." Mary hadn't unlocked the front entrance since she and Elijah had both come in early, too early for the practice to be open.

He nodded and got to his feet. "Sounds good."

"I brought brownies and a pumpkin roll," she told him. "Both go well with coffee or tea."

Elijah gave her a small smile and then waited for her to precede him. Mary understood that he was in a bit of a bind with Beatrice out and Diana gone. She passed by and immediately went into the break room where she made coffee and opened the soft-plastic container of treats from the counter, setting it in the middle of the table along with two paper plates. Then, as the coffee continued to drip, she pulled the pot during the process and poured her employer a cup of coffee and placed it in front of where he usually sat. Out of habit, she put out creamer and sugar as well as napkins. The scent of the coffee and a hint of chocolate from the brownies permeated the air in the break room as her boss entered, making her feel self-conscious. The strength of his presence unnerved her. She concentrated on the task at hand, which was fixing herself a hot drink. When she turned, she watched as he took in the table, especially the baked treats sitting in the middle.

He sat down and then reached for a chocolate brownie, closing his eyes as he took his first bite. "This is delicious."

Mary felt herself relax. "I like to bake. Have you ever had this before?" she asked, gesturing toward the layer of pumpkin cake she'd spread with cream cheese icing before rolling it into a wonderful bit of round tastiness.

He smiled. "I have. I'm going to eat a small piece of that next."

Mary was glad to see he enjoyed the delicious treats. "It's one of my favorites. I love the cream cheese filling."

After sampling a brownie and the pumpkin roll, Mary glanced at the clock and stood, ready to assist him during this difficult time. "If you'd like, I can check the file cabinet to see if there is any information about the agency Beatrice uses to hire vet assistants."

"Yes, please." Then he stood as he drank the last bit of his coffee.

She set her mug in the sink. "If I can't find anything, I'll call Beatrice."

"It's not necessary to bother her," he said. "I'll figure it out."

Mary went to the front office to dig through the front desk cabinets and discovered some promising notes. She withdrew the folder and brought it to Elijah in his office. "There is mention of a vet tech school here that helps to place its graduates. Would you like me to call and arrange interviews for you?"

He accepted the file from her. "I'll reach out to them."

She noticed a sudden change in his demeanor. He had become quiet and withdrawn once again. Was the stress getting to him? "Please let me know if you change your mind."

He nodded as Mary stifled a yawn unsuccessfully. "Sorry," she said when she saw that he continued to watch her as if to take her measure.

"Didn't sleep well?" he said gruffly.

"I'm fine," she assured him. "I was up a little early this morning, is all."

He frowned. "Sleep in tomorrow. You don't need to bring

in breakfast. I'll eat something at home tomorrow and buy lunch for us both."

"That's not necessary—"

"It is. I don't want you getting sick due to lack of sleep." He narrowed his eyes. "You're the only one here to help, Mary. Please let me take care of tomorrow. I was going to buy lunch today, but I didn't take your delicious casserole home, and there's a lot of it left."

Mary was touched by his offer to bring in food. "That's nice of you," she said, "but you don't have to do that. I like to cook and bake." She studied him with concern, noting that he had dark shadows under his eyes. "Are you taking care of yourself?"

"I haven't been sleeping well," he admitted. "I'm stressed about finding the right person to replace Diana."

"I have a feeling that everything will be okay through your staff changes," she murmured. "And I'll help in any way I can." Mary wondered about his reasons for becoming a veterinarian. "What made you decide to become a vet?"

Elijah smiled, his blue eyes brightening. "I love animals, and it felt natural for me to want to help them whenever they were sick or hurt."

"That's why I enjoy working here. I love animals and love to pet them. I also enjoy chatting with their owners." She'd always wanted a dog, but she never asked her parents if they could get one. And as it turned out it was a good thing since she wouldn't have been able to take a pet to her grandparents' house when her grandfather become ill.

"You ever have a pet?" he asked softly.

Mary shook her head. "No, never."

"But you'd like to have one someday?" Elijah sat back in his chair as he studied her.

"I don't know if it's possible, but I would," she admitted. "Someday."

He stood. "I hope you get your wish one day."

Mary smiled without commenting. She picked up his cup to wash in the sink. "I'll leave the brownies on the counter and the pumpkin roll in the refrigerator. Help yourself whenever you want any." She was delightfully surprised when he lingered instead of escaping to his office. She faced him, noting the slight upward curve of his mouth. "Let me know if you need anything."

"Thanks," he said. "I'll be in my office." She saw him glance at his watch. "Time to open up."

She nodded as she set the clean wet cups in the sink rack. As she turned, she saw him exit into the hall. "Elijah?"

He stopped. "Yes?"

"Try not to worry," she told him. "Everything will be fine."

He held her gaze for a brief moment before he inclined his head and left.

Chapter Five

"Hello, Mr. Beauregard, how are you?" Mary greeted him with a smile at the clinic the next day. "Who is this with you?"

"This is my daughter Catherine's guinea pig," the older man said, holding up the fluffy white-and-brown animal. "She just bought him, and I wanted to make sure Bruiser here is healthy."

Mary nodded as she studied the pet's adorable reddish-brown face with his dark eyes and white whiskers on each side of his cute little pink nose. "Good idea. It's best to bring Bruiser in for annual checkups. Dr. Zook can also give you some advice on what to look for so her guinea pig stays well." She stood. "I'll let him know you're here. Please have a seat until I call you."

The man nodded and sat close to the right of the reception window.

Just before she turned toward the back, she saw the notification come up for a new email. She checked it quickly and saw the résumés of potential vet techs Elijah was waiting for. He'd called the vet school yesterday after she'd located Beatrice's files for him, and he'd been looking at potential candidates. Only two came through.

He looked up as she entered. "Mr. Beauregard is here with a new patient for you. His daughter's new guinea pig."

Elijah stood. "You can bring Mr. Beauregard and…"

Mary had to stifle a smile. "Bruiser."

He chuckled. "Thanks. You can bring him into exam room two as soon as he's ready." When she didn't immediately leave, Elijah looked up at her with questioning blue eyes.

"The résumés you wanted came in." She'd forward them to him so he could take a look.

"Wonderful!" he said. "Thanks."

She felt pleased by his good humor. "You're welcome. If there is anything else I can do…"

"You're doing plenty," he told her. "I'll wait until you get Mr. Beauregard and Bruiser in the room before I head in."

Mary nodded and then went back to escort Bruiser and his owner into the exam room. These mood swings of Elijah confused her, making her feel uncomfortable when he was grumpy or irritable. Still, she enjoyed times like this when he seemed pleased by her work.

From that point on, the day grew busier. Without Diana or Beatrice to help, Mary wondered how they would cope until a new vet tech was hired. By the time the last patient left, she felt exhausted. But she didn't complain. There was something wonderful about getting work done.

After she locked up the door, she returned to her desk and entered the day's patients into her computer.

Elijah came into her area as she was shutting down for the day. "It was crazy today," he said with a tired smile. "We have an easier patient load next week, so I've scheduled an interview for Monday." He paused and studied her intently. "Did you eat one of the breakfast sandwiches I brought this morning?"

She shook her head. "I got involved in the books, and then your patients started arriving."

"You haven't eaten today?" he said, his voice sharpening.

Mary blinked at his tone. "I had a cruller before I came

into work. We're shorthanded. I didn't want to stop to eat and let you down."

His expression softened. "Let's check out the schedule for Tuesday and Wednesday as well. If it looks overwhelming, reschedule the annuals to allow for a lunch break but keep the same time slots for the appointments that need to be seen because of a problem. I don't want you going without food."

Warmed by his concern for her well-being, she opened her mouth to tell him it was all right but then changed her mind. "Okay," she replied quietly because she did need to eat if she was to continue at the hectic pace Diana's and Beatrice's absences had created. And a few days ago, she had promised her parents she'd talk with her boss about changing her hours— not something she was looking forward to at this point.

Elijah met Mary's gaze as she entered his office on Tuesday morning the following week. His patient had left over a half hour ago. "Betty Thomas is here for her interview," she told him.

"Thank you, Mary." He closed her file and set it to one side. "Would you please bring her back?"

Mary, who'd surprised him all last week with her efficiency and kindness on the job, nodded and then left. She returned within a minute with the woman he might hire depending on her knowledge and qualifications…and the way she handled herself.

Betty Thomas was older than he'd realized, but, in his opinion, that might be a plus in her favor. Dark hair cut short, she appeared to be in her late forties. She seemed nervous as she sat across from him.

"Thank you for coming, Betty," he said as he met her gaze with a smile. "Tell me about yourself. Why did you go to school to become a vet tech?"

Betty tucked a strand of salt-and-pepper hair behind her ear, then proceeded to tell him about her love of animals and how she was trained as a tech but loved grooming. He decided that if he hired her, he'd make use of both sets of skills.

"Wonderful." He smiled and asked a few more questions. When he wrapped up the interview, he said, "Thanks for coming in. I'll give you a call in a day or so."

She stood. "Thank you for the opportunity," she murmured as he accompanied her to the front entrance.

Elijah nodded. "I'm glad we met."

"Have a good day, Dr. Zook," she said. Then she left.

He turned and saw Mary watching him from behind the reception counter. "She may be a good addition to our staff. She has her tech license and she's an experienced groomer." He walked through the door and eyed Mary where she sat at her computer. He sighed. "I'll use her as a full-time tech and a groomer when needed. But I'm thinking I need more than one full-time vet assistant."

"That sounds like a good idea," Mary said.

He smiled. "I'll be in my office." Beatrice usually did the hiring so having to handle it was challenging for him. The only thing he'd had to do was to hire Beatrice, and that was easy because someone had highly recommended her, which he knew now was a wonderful assessment of her skill set and intelligence.

Seated at his desk, he checked his day's schedule. It wasn't too bad today, and he'd already asked Mary to lighten the load for the next two days. But he couldn't go with a light schedule for long. He still had loans to pay and the cost of rent, utilities and other items related to this building as well as at home.

"Elijah?" Mary stood in the open doorway. "I just spoke with Beatrice. She gave me the name of the placement coordinator of another vet tech school." She approached with a sheet of paper.

Learning that Mary had spoken with Beatrice upset him. He had told Mary not to bother Beatrice, and she'd ignored him. "What did I tell you about bothering Beatrice?"

"But I—"

"Mary, Beatrice is dealing with her ill sister," he interrupted briskly. "That's why I didn't want you to call her." He frowned. "We have a light afternoon. Why don't you head on home?"

"Dr. Zook, I know what you said, but I—"

"We'll talk about it another time," he said, still upset. Moments later, he saw Mary walk past his office on her way out.

She should have listened to him. She was a good employee, which was why it bothered him that she'd called Beatrice despite his telling her not to. It was better if she left now anyway. It was too late and too dark when she usually left, which wasn't a safe time to be driving alone near the side of the road in a horse-drawn buggy.

The woman confused him and made him act irrationally at times. Elijah sighed and closed his eyes. He knew he'd been short with her, and he felt bad about it. It was difficult to keep the clinic on track with his staffing issues. His hectic work life and what happened to him as a child made him closed off. He didn't trust easily, yet he'd answered Mary's questions about his reasons for becoming a vet, and she'd talked about her love for animals, one of the reasons for enjoying her job here.

Overcome with a sudden headache, Elijah rubbed his temples in an attempt to relieve it. His disappointment and his last conversation with Mary had hit him hard. The last thing he needed was to drive her away. Tomorrow he had to find a way to make things right with her.

Chapter Six

"What are you doing home so early?" her mother asked as Mary entered the house.

Mary scowled. "Dr. Zook sent me home. Said we weren't busy enough for me to stay, but that's not the truth."

Joanna Troyer frowned. "What do you mean it's not the truth?"

"I told you Diana left to get married so she could move from the area with her military husband," she said.

"*Ja.*" Mam stirred batter in the bowl before her on the countertop. "So why did he ask you to leave?"

"He thinks I called Beatrice and asked for help after he told me not to bother her," Mary said, feeling hurt and frustrated. "I didn't call her, but he wouldn't listen. He cut me off before I could explain. Diana called Beatrice, who then called me to check in and offer advice for Diana's replacement."

"Hmm," her mother said. "Sounds like someone must have betrayed him in the past."

Mary felt a jolt. "You think so?"

"It's a *gut* possibility, *dochter.* A man who is quick to respond the way he did must have surely suffered in the past." Her *mam* paused in her stirring to add milk to the batter. "When you return tomorrow, be easy. Don't let him see how upset you were by his attitude. He'll figure it out in time and will feel bad for jumping to conclusions."

"*Oll recht.*" Mary grabbed an apron and tied it around her waist. "What do you want me to do to help with supper?"

"I thought we'd have fried chicken, corn casserole and home fries with fresh rolls." Her mother smiled at her. "Want to peel potatoes?"

"Sure." As she worked, Mary attempted to banish from her mind her employer's angry tirade against her for something she didn't do.

Tomorrow was a new day. If things didn't get better between Elijah and her before the weekend, she wasn't sure what she was going to do.

Usually, the main meal in the Amish household was at midday, but with her job and her brother Simeon's new part-time employment at Kings General Store, her mother had deemed supper the time for the larger meal instead of simply sandwiches or other light fare, which worked out well for everyone.

During each afternoon, her father took time to visit the *dawdi haus* to see if her grandparents needed anything. Dat always went over with the excuse of bringing them one baked good or another, telling them that their daughter had made too much food. While there, he also made sure that her *gross-daddi* wasn't tempted to do something that would put him at risk for falling or hurting himself.

Mary's *grosseldre* were always invited to join them for a meal, but they preferred to remain in their small home, so her mother usually brought them supper before the rest of her family sat down to eat.

Later that night, after the supper dishes were washed and dried, her mother came to her. "Why don't you invite Dr. Zook over for a meal? Find out which day works for him, and we'll ensure there is a place set for him."

And it would be one way for her parents to meet the man,

she thought, recalling her mother's insistence the other day that it was time the family met her boss. "Mam, I don't know if he'll even be talking with me tomorrow," Mary said with concern. "I can't ask him yet. Maybe after I know for sure that things are *oll recht* between us first."

"I'll leave the when up to you," Mam said, "but I think it will be nice for him to have a home-cooked meal with our family. Show him that he's appreciated for the work he does for the community."

Mary nodded, grateful that her mother was leaving it up to her. "I'll let you know."

As she drove to work the next morning, Mary tried not to worry how the day would go. Her mother had made enough dinner rolls that there were plenty for her to take into the clinic after she'd brought a few over to her grandparents. She also brought in a jar of homemade peach jam and four of the iced cinnamon buns she'd made late last night to snack on during the day. As she'd told her boss recently, she loved to cook and bake…and share whatever she made with others. She enjoyed seeing Elijah find pleasure in her food.

Her stomach burned with anxiety as she parked in the barn behind the building and tied up her mare inside. She filled the horse water trough before she headed to the clinic. She'd come back to check on Bess later. There was no sign of Dr. Zook's car. Taking a deep breath, Mary unlocked the door and entered the silent building. She set the plate of rolls on the break room table, then put the peach jam and cinnamon buns in the refrigerator before grabbing water. After turning on the coffeepot, she went to her desk and booted up her computer.

She worked to get caught up on updating the patient medical charts and relaxed as she became immersed in that job before switching to bookkeeping to add this week's receipts.

Shortly after, she heard the door open and shut, and Elijah's footsteps down the hall to his office.

She concentrated on her computer work. She hoped today would be smoother than yesterday. Mary felt his presence before he spoke.

"Would you come back into my office?" Elijah said gently.

Palms sweaty, she nodded and went to confront him.

"You needed something?" she asked politely.

Elijah looked up from his desk. "Yes, have a seat, Mary."

She sat and waited. He seemed more relaxed than yesterday. "I... Can I help you with something?"

Elijah gazed at her as if he was deciding what to do with her.

"Dr. Zook—"

He raised his hand to stop her. "I owe you an apology for my behavior yesterday," he said, much to her surprise.

"It's okay." Mary never expected him to apologize and felt relieved that he did so. "I need you to know that I didn't call Beatrice. She called me." She tried to gauge his reaction when he eyed her silently.

The man released a heavy sigh. "I know." His blue eyes filled with regret. "I realized you wouldn't go against what I told you. I should have known better. I'm sorry that I didn't give you a chance to explain."

"You've been under a lot of pressure," she said, "and I haven't been much help."

Elijah shook his head. "On the contrary, you've been more helpful than you know."

"Thank you," she said softly. "I appreciate that." Mary rose. "Did you see the dinner rolls in the break room? They're good. My mother made them last evening. You can warm them if you want in the microwave."

He smiled. "Sounds delicious." He held her gaze again. "Thank you, Mary."

Relieved, she nodded as she returned his grin. "Why not get something to eat before your first patient arrives?"

The rolls were good. He ate two of them in his office but didn't give into the temptation of another. Thinking about Mary's smile, Elijah was amazed by the woman's ability to forgive quickly. He'd been angry with her when he'd had no right to be. She'd tried to explain after he'd accused her of calling Beatrice, but he hadn't allowed her to talk. And that was on him.

He had quickly realized he'd misjudged her after he'd forced her to leave early. Everything Mary had done in the office to date had been to ensure things ran smoothly in Beatrice's absence. He'd judged too quickly, something he'd promised himself he'd never do since he was a young boy whose entire family had been judged unfairly. He promised himself that he'd be better going forward.

"So far, I want to hire Betty," he said later after he'd gone with his coffee to the front desk to talk with her. "And I've decided it's best to have another vet tech working here too." This would allow staff to cover each other. Besides he now had enough work for two techs.

"At least, you'll have Betty now," she replied.

Elijah nodded. "Yes, I need to call her with a job offer. If she accepts, I'll set up a time for her to come in for the paperwork."

"Would you like me to call her?" Mary asked.

"I'll do it, but thanks." He finished the last of his coffee. "Time to get to work. And thanks for bringing in food again." He'd been surviving on dry cereal and frozen meals at home, so he greatly appreciated all the wonderful food she brought in to share.

"You're welcome." She smiled. "I'd better unlock the door." Mary got up from the chair. "If you need me for anything, please let me know."

Today was a light day, so he should be fine handling the scheduled appointments that were left.

Around noon, someone rushed into the office with an extremely ill Pomeranian. Mary came to his office to tell him. The woman was babysitting the dog for her daughter, who was away at college.

"I don't know if Sweetness ate something she shouldn't have," Vicki Keller said, sounding anxious. "I didn't leave anything around for her to get into. I've had pets. I'm always careful."

With a reassuring smile, Elijah accepted the dog carrier from the woman. "Let me take a look at her."

"Oh, look at her!" Mary said softly.

Elijah knew how she felt. The Pomeranian was considered a toy breed with thick reddish-brown fur and tiny pointed ears with black eyes and small nose. Mary looked as if she wanted to take him out of his small kennel to hold and pet him. "Try not to worry," he told Vicki. "I'll do what I can for her."

"Thank you!" The woman's brown eyes filled with tears. She looked to be in her early fifties, with short chestnut brown hair cut just above her nape.

"Why don't you have a seat?" Mary suggested with compassionate understanding. "Sweetness is in good hands. May I get you a cup of tea or coffee?"

Elijah looked approvingly at Mary. "I'll let you know whatever I find out after I examine her," he told Vicki. He was amazed by how much of a calming influence the Amish woman had on the owners and guardians of ill or hurt pets brought into the clinic.

He carried the dog to the back and began his examination. As he pressed on certain areas on Sweetness's stomach, she yelped as if in pain. He would have to do an X-ray and an ultrasound to see if there was a blockage of some kind. If she needed surgery, he'd have a problem as he didn't have a skilled assistant to help him.

He placed Sweetness carefully in a kennel and went to talk with Mrs. Keller. "Vicki, I'm going to do an X-ray and some other tests on Sweetness. I'll be back to talk with you. This could take a while. I won't do anything without your consent."

"Can we reach your daughter for her consent, if needed?" Mary asked.

"Yes." The woman appeared concerned. "I can call her. She'll be home next week for Thanksgiving."

"Try not to worry," Mary said soothingly. "Dr. Zook is good at what he does."

Elijah felt a rush a pleasure at Mary's belief in his abilities.

Vicki looked distraught. "Could she have gotten into something in my house?"

"Did you find her eating anything she shouldn't have?" Elijah kept his voice soft as he spoke with her. The woman shook her head. "Okay. I should have more information for you in a half hour or so."

"Thank you." The woman's brown eyes glistened with tears. She folded her arms across her stomach.

"Would you like a cup of tea?" Mary asked, and Elijah was grateful for her quick thinking in offering the woman comfort.

"Yes, black tea with sugar if you have. Thank you," Vicki said.

"Try not to worry, okay?" he said. "Try to relax and I'll be back as soon as I can."

She nodded. A few moments later, he paused by the break room and saw Mary making the woman's tea. "This isn't a good time to be without a vet tech."

"I...have an idea," Mary told him. "Beatrice told me where to call for a temporary assistant while you search for someone permanent."

"Where?" he asked, then he waved his query off. "Never mind, it doesn't matter. If you'd do whatever Beatrice told you, I'd be grateful." He rubbed his temples where a throbbing told him he was getting a headache. "Let me know what you learn."

"I will." Mary left with the tea for Vicki, then returned to the break room with a bottle of acetaminophen and a bottle of water. "Here," she said as she shook two into her hand. "These may help your headache."

He blinked. "How did you know?"

"It's easy to see that you're in pain," she said. "I'll make a phone call to see what I can do to find someone to help you." She bit her lip. "I wish I could do more," she murmured.

Pleased by her concern for him and her willingness to pitch in, Elijah accepted the water and took the two pills.

Setting the bottle of water down, he checked on his patient. He needed to get images to help him determine how best to treat the young Pomeranian. He only hoped Mary's solution would get him the help he needed today.

Mary pulled the sheet of paper from her top desk drawer of the information Beatrice had given her and studied it. What if no one was available to help? What could she do then?

The phone on her desk rang twice before Mary answered it. "Zook Veterinary Clinic. My name is Mary. How may I help you?"

"Mary, it's Beatrice," the familiar female voice said from the other end of the line.

"Beatrice! How is your sister?" she asked. Hearing her voice brought a bit of comfort. Beatrice was a pleasing woman with skills that made the office and the clinic work efficiently.

"She's doing better," Beatrice said. "But it's going to be a long road for her with chemo treatments and whatever reactions she has to the cancer meds. She'll begin treatment as soon as she's recovered from her surgery."

"I'm so sorry," Mary said. "Please know that I'll keep Carol in my prayers. It's good that she has you to take care of her."

"Thanks, Mary," the woman replied. "I know it's been hard for you in the office."

"We're doing fine. Please don't think a moment more about it." Mary sat back in her desk chair.

"Have you called for a temporary tech yet?" the manager asked. "If not, why don't you let me handle it? I know most everyone at the New Berne Animal Hospital, and I'll call to let you know when to expect someone."

"I hate to put you out," Mary began. She didn't want Beatrice to focus on the clinic, and she knew Dr. Zook wouldn't like that either.

"It's no bother," Beatrice said. "It's the least I can do. Carol is still sleeping a lot. I'll make the call as soon the hospital opens."

Mary leaned toward the desk. "If you're sure—"

"Absolutely," Beatrice reassured her. "Carol won't be up until ten, at the earliest. She sleeps a lot right now."

"Thanks, Beatrice. I appreciate this." Mary felt relieved by Beatrice's offer of assistance.

"I'm glad I can help, especially with you handling a double workload." Beatrice sighed. "I feel bad for leaving you in the lurch."

"You taught me well. I don't feel pressured," Mary said. "Diana's departure was the most difficult part, especially for Elijah." She bit her lip for allowing the use of his first name to slip out. Thankfully, Beatrice didn't seem to notice. She simply promised again to call Mary back.

Mary took the cinnamon buns from the refrigerator and put them on the table in her attempt to put Elijah in a better mood. She smiled as she recalled Elijah's enjoyment of anything sweet she baked. He always finished the snacks she brought in, and it made her happy to see how much he savored each sugary bite. But he also liked the sandwiches and casserole she'd brought early in this week, so he was one to eat more than just snacks.

Twenty minutes later, Beatrice called again.

"Good news," the older woman said. "The vet I spoke with has agreed to loan Elijah an assistant for a few weeks."

"Thank you, Beatrice. But you need to worry about your sister, not us here in the office," Mary said.

"It's just a few phone calls, Mary," Beatrice replied. "Call me if you need to, and maybe let me know once someone is hired, okay?"

Mary agreed, feeling better about the state of the office during Beatrice's absence. A vet tech, even a temporary one, would relieve some of the daily stress put on Elijah, who would need help with surgeries and other complicated procedures as well as simple exams, although Mary could always hold an animal on the exam table during a routine physical, which usually included vaccines. They'd worked well together when Fluffball had been brought in and she was sure they could be a team like that again.

Mary smiled when Elijah entered the front desk area after she hung up the phone. "How's Sweetness?" she asked.

"I managed to take X-rays. I need to look at the films and do an ultrasound before I decide on a treatment plan for her." He looked concerned. "The Pomeranian was docile while I took the images, which concerns me. It's clear she's in a great deal of pain."

"Vicki is still waiting," Mary told him. "Maybe you can bring her up-to-date and suggest she go home and wait for your call."

Elijah nodded and she watched as he entered the waiting room to talk with the woman. Vicki looked worried, Mary thought, but the longer Elijah spoke with her, Vicki appeared less stressed. She saw her nod and then put on her coat.

"Someone should be here in a while to assist you," Mary said once Elijah had returned to the front desk. "Beatrice called in again and offered to assist in finding temporary help. Her sister is still sleeping," she explained quickly, "and she has time on her hands. She said someone will be here today to help."

Elijah studied her, making her feel self-conscious for a moment. She reached up a hand to see if a stray hair had come loose from her chignon, but everything seemed to be in place.

"Thanks," he finally said. "I know you yourself would have made the call, but Beatrice is one determined woman, so I'm not surprised that she insisted on helping."

"Yes," Mary said with a nod. "She feels bad for leaving us in the lurch. I told her we were fine, that I can handle the job at hand because she taught me well." She smiled. "She sounded relieved." She leaned against the chair back. "If you get hungry, there are cinnamon rolls on the table. You can eat them as they are or warm them in the microwave."

He grinned, and she caught her breath at how much he

affected her when his face lit up. "I'm going to take a look at Sweetness's images before I check next week's schedule."

"It may be a busy couple of days before the holiday," she warned him. "But not as hectic as it could be since we rescheduled some appointments until the week after."

"I'm sure we'll manage, especially if I get some help," Elijah said with a soft expression, and she shifted under his gaze. "Thank you, Mary."

She returned his smile. "You're welcome."

He left to return to his office. Mary watched him go, thinking how glad she was that he seemed to be in better spirits today and was no longer upset with her.

Her mother's suspicion came back to haunt her. *Someone in his past must have betrayed him,* Mary thought.

She couldn't help but wonder if that was true...and if so, who.

Chapter Seven

Elijah entered the break room and poured himself another coffee. He then plated a roll and put it in the microwave for a few seconds. The scent of the pastry was wonderful as he pulled it out warm. He brought coffee and roll into his office and sat down. After taking a sip of coffee, he leaned back in his chair and closed his eyes for a brief moment. When he opened them again, he glanced around the empty room, looking forward to the time when he no longer had to worry about staffing. Elijah knew that he would pay the best rate because it was necessary to hold on to good help.

Mary showed up in the doorway. "Vicki Keller is back for Sweetness."

"Tell her I'll be right out." He took one long sip of coffee before he stood.

She'd quickly left to let Vicki know.

His next patient wasn't due to arrive for another hour. He headed to the waiting area to give Vicki the dog's medication along with instructions for her care. The woman was relieved that Sweetness would be all right.

Then he returned to leisurely sip his coffee and enjoy another cinnamon bun. He'd finished both when Mary entered, likely ready to take her own coffee break before their next patient.

He nodded as she entered, then said impulsively, "I'll order lunch later today. Any sign of the temporary vet tech yet?"

"I'm afraid not," Mary said. "Do you want me to call Beatrice and ask when we can expect someone since she made the arrangements?"

Elijah shook his head. "No need. I'm sure the tech will arrive eventually." He sighed wearily, feeling heavy from poor sleep and worry over the clinic being understaffed. A short time later, a soft bell sounded in the break room, signaling that someone had entered the waiting area. "I believe my next patient is here."

Mary nodded. "Mr. Wellsy's dog Benjy. I'll go check him in," she said before she left the room.

Mary was eager for the vet tech to arrive to help with Benjy's surgery to remove a lump. She considered calling the New Berne Animal Hospital to follow up, but before she could dial, the front door opened and a man entered. He approached her desk, his gaze intent, and looked a bit startled when he caught sight of her.

"Hello, may I help you?" Mary asked.

The man nodded. "I'm Jacob and I'm here to assist Elijah Zook today."

"I'll let him know—"

"No need," Jacob said, surprising her. "We know each other. I'll just go back and annouce myself."

"But—"

"It's all right." The man opened the door to the hallway where the exam rooms were located, then strode briskly toward the back room.

Mary hurried to follow him, but then froze when, in response to Jacob's greeting, she heard Elijah say, "What are you doing here?"

Mary went back to her desk. Would Elijah be upset with her for allowing the man to slip by her? She closed her eyes and took several deep calming breaths. She would find out soon enough. To her surprise, there were no complaints from her boss, and after fifteen minutes passed with silence in the back, she assumed all was well.

In the meantime, she saw new résumés come through from the vet school they'd contacted, which was good news for the clinic.

Jacob entered the front area as Mary opened the candidates' applications, intending to print them for Dr. Zook. "Elijah said I needed to ask you if I can have a cinnamon roll before I take one," Jacob said with a pout. Mary wondered how the man knew Elijah since Jacob had gone into the back without an invitation and Elijah hadn't come out to scold her for allowing him through.

Mary chuckled. "Help yourself. I brought four and they are big ones."

"Oh, and Elijah said to call Benjy's owner to have him picked up about 3:00 p.m." Jacob turned to leave, then halted and faced her. "Thank you in advance for the cinnamon roll."

She nodded. "There should be coffee left." Mary saw the next patient and owner through the front door before they entered. She recognized the woman immediately. "Jacob," she said as he turned to leave. "Would you please let Dr. Zook know that Mrs. Decker is here with his next patient?"

"Will do," Jacob said.

Elijah walked in moments later from the back of the clinic and stepped into the waiting room. "Good morning, Mrs. Decker. I see you have Cuddles with you."

Mary watched as the woman followed Elijah, carrying the gray tabby's carrier down the hall into an exam room.

Jacob then entered the reception area again. "A vet tech

named Lacey will be here instead of me on Monday," he said with a smile.

"You know Dr. Zook," she commented as she studied him. Why did Jacob look familiar?

"I certainly do," he replied with amusement. His lips twitched. "Eli is my brother."

Mary felt her face heat. "Oh! Beatrice didn't tell me."

Jacob grinned. "I'm an equine vet. I also treat other animals at the New Berne Animal Hospital. I was off today and stopped by my office briefly. When Beatrice called and said that Eli needed help, I figured I'd assist him for the day. Sometimes it's fun to bug your brother, you know?"

She laughed, now seeing the resemblance. His hair was darker than Elijah's but his eyes were the same blue color. Studying him, she recognized that he had the same nose and mouth as her boss's. "I know what you mean. I have two brothers."

Jacob smiled, assessing her.

"What?" she said.

"Beatrice didn't tell me about you either." He shook his head. "I never would have thought."

"I don't understand." Mary frowned.

He suddenly grinned. "Nothing. I'm glad you've been here to help Elijah. I told him more than once that he needed to hire two assistants." His expression sobered. "I better get back there."

"Did you enjoy your cinnamon roll?" she asked.

His blue eyes lit up. "I did. Delicious! I may have to come here more often to sample more of your baked goods." He ran his fingers through his dark hair. "Thanks, Mary."

She smiled, deciding she liked him. He seemed more easygoing than his brother, but something about Elijah affected her in ways she didn't understand. She knew she shouldn't think about Elijah as anyone other her boss and an Englisher, but she admired his love of animals and his dedication in caring for them, even while handling the stress he'd been under. Her mother's insistence that he come to supper came to mind but she wasn't sure having him at their house and seated at their kitchen table was a good idea. And the idea made her nervous. Still, she had to take her *mam*'s feelings into account.

Patients came and went. A huge chef salad with bread was delivered, and the staff ate when they found time.

Mary printed résumés from the vet school, emailed by Hart University. She looked them over, made a few notations on sticky notes on each one, placed them on Elijah's desk for him to peruse later and returned to her desk.

Hours later, Jacob came out from the back. "Heading out, Mary. It was nice to meet you."

"Nice to meet you, too, Jacob." She watched him exit through the front door, the same way he'd come in. Having him in the office today gave her a tiny peek into Elijah Zook's background.

Remembering her mother's suggestion that Elijah come to dinner, she headed back to his office, where she was sure he'd be alone.

She approached him hesitantly. "Elijah?"

He glanced up from his computer. "Yes?"

Under his scrutiny, she swallowed hard. "My mother… she wants you to come to supper one day. Since next weekend is Thanksgiving, maybe you could come another time?"

Elijah didn't say anything at first, as if trying to determine the right thing to say. "Maybe. We'll have to see."

"My mother is an excellent cook." When his only further response was a nod and nothing more, Mary felt disappointed. She shouldn't feel that way but she did. He wouldn't commit to joining her family for a meal, and she couldn't make him.

But the worst thing was having to tell her mother about her boss's unwillingness to say yes to the invitation.

Elijah had been startled when Mary invited him for a meal with her family. He'd have to think about it. It was nice of her mother, but would he be comfortable in an Amish household? Ever since the shunning, he'd been hesitant to interact with any of the Amish in New Berne. As an equine and large animal vet, his brother Jacob frequently had Amish clients, as members of their community called him to care for their horses and other large farm animals. Aaron and his father interacted with them but only professionally from time to time in their furniture business. His mother did mending for Englishers but not for the Amish, and she was content with that, as the shunning still affected her. Elijah had also kept himself apart from the New Berne community until Mary. She was the first one he'd dealt with, and he'd felt forced to work with her since Beatrice had hired her. Still, Mary turned out to be a pleasant surprise, and he enjoyed seeing her each day at the clinic. Her work ethic, her calming presence and her ability to recognize small details, like when he had a headache, as well as her spot-on intuition at times made her easy to get along with. He would have been lost without her in the office, and he needed to make sure nothing stopped her from coming in.

Mary appeared at the door a little while later. "Elijah? I'm going to head home."

Jacob had left but Elijah was still surprised by how late it was. "Be careful going home," he said.

She nodded and turned to leave.

"Mary?" he called out. "I don't like you driving in and then home in the dark. I think we should adjust your hours. You've been coming in early and leaving late."

"Oh." She appeared surprised and then relieved. "What hours do you want me to work?"

He'd given it some thought. "Eight or nine until four as long as it's light outside. We can talk more about it tomorrow."

She smiled. "Okay. Have a nice evening, Elijah."

"Same to you." He watched her leave and was glad he'd suggested changing her hours. Until now, he hadn't been thinking clearly. Lack of sleep had delayed his common sense.

He leaned back in his chair, stretching, before he turned off his computer. Then he stood and put on his coat, turned off all the lights and left, locking up behind him. Elijah was surprised to see snow in the parking lot behind his clinic, enough to have already covered the pavement and his car. When he'd checked earlier, the evening's weather forecast called for flurries without any accumulation.

After cleaning off the windows, Elijah got into his vehicle. Mary had just left and would be driving home in this mess. As he pulled onto the road, the snow fell harder but he saw faint snow-covered buggy tracks in his headlights. Concerned, he continued to follow them, and he noticed at one point they disappeared altogether. The road was dangerous for buggies, especially in the dark. He turned up the speed of his windshield wipers and searched the road and shoulder carefully. And hoped there was no cause for him to worry about her not making it home safely. As the snowstorm worsened, he offered up a silent prayer for her safety as he drove on slowly with growing uneasiness.

Chapter Eight

Mary hadn't expected the snow. It was bad enough driving home in the dark but with the roads covered, it made driving her buggy more dangerous. The headlights on her vehicle showed an increase in the rate of snowfall. She'd turned on her windshield wipers as soon as she climbed into her vehicle. When she'd seen the snow, before leaving the office, she'd debated whether she should ask Elijah to follow her to her house. In the end, she'd decided she'd be fine heading home since her house wasn't too far away. But as she drove on, the distance seemed much longer than it had that morning.

She strained to see, her heartbeat increasing with worry at the whiteout in her headlights. Mary glimpsed the bright lights of a vehicle as it approached from a distance behind her. She was on the shoulder of the road so the driver should be able to pass her without incident. But then suddenly the car was upon her, speeding when it should have been slowing down on the slippery, snow-covered road. The driver must not have seen her, despite the buggy's running lights. The automobile swerved at the last minute, skidding briefly onto the shoulder before pulling back onto the road. She felt a jolt as her frightened horse reared up and bolted. She gasped as she bumped her head against the dashboard as the mare raced off the road through a ditch and kept going. Mary tried to rein in the animal, but the terrified mare continued to gallop several yards, dragging the buggy with it before finally coming to an abrupt stop in a farmer's field.

Stunned, her head throbbing, she wondered what to do next. She slid open the buggy door on the driver's side. As she climbed out, she slid on the snow but soon found her footing. She went to the front to check on her horse, calming the animal with soft tones until the animal settled. Then she circled her carriage. It was hard to tell in the driving snow if her horse was injured or if her buggy had gotten damaged, but they both seemed okay to her. After the warmth of heat inside her buggy, the frigid cold and wind made her gasp as snow covered her bonnet and black woolen cape and entered her shoes.

What to do, she thought. *What to do!*

First, she needed to find her cell phone. She hadn't thought about it until now, but she knew it hadn't been on the seat beside her when she got out of the buggy to check the horse. The jolt when they'd gone off the road must have tossed it to the floor.

Mary started to shiver and couldn't stop herself. Knowing that she needed to get out of the cold, she went back inside her vehicle, where she hoped it would still be warm. The windshield wipers continued to swish back and forth across the front glass, and the headlights were on, so the battery was still working. She tried to climb into the buggy, but then she suddenly felt woozy and fell backward in the snow. *Please, Lord, help me!* She prayed as she struggled to her feet, chilled to the bone, her hands now red from the cold. *I need to get inside and look for my cell phone so that I can call for help!* But her next attempt to get up was unsuccessful. Her head hurt where she'd hit it on the dashboard and she lay on the snow until she garnered enough strength to stand.

Mary heard the roar of an engine as another vehicle approached traveling slowly in deference to the weather and road conditions. She watched with trepidation as it drew close and slowed down before the driver pulled onto the shoulder next to her buggy in the field. Frightened because she didn't know who it was, she took a step back as if she could somehow hide, hugging herself to get control of the shaking.

The driver opened the door and a man climbed out. "Mary?"

She immediately relaxed when she saw it was Dr. Zook who'd stopped to help her. "Elijah?"

"Yes, it's me." He looked concerned as he approached. "Are you all right?"

"Not really." But she felt hope rise at his arrival. "What are you doing here?"

Elijah clicked on a flashlight he must have taken from his car so he could better see her. "After you left, I locked up and saw that it was snowing. I wanted to make sure you got home safely."

"Thank you," she said in a trembly voice. "A car driving too fast spooked my horse and then clipped the buggy as it went by. The driver didn't even stop."

"Why don't you wait in my car," Elijah invited. "The heat is on, and it's toasty inside." His expression darkened when he studied her in the battery lamplight. "You hit your forehead. You have a scrape and it's starting to swell." He came closer and examined her forehead. "Come on. I have a blanket in the back seat. Let's get you warm before I assess the damage to your horse and buggy."

Mary was grateful when he helped her to his car and opened the door. Gesturing her inside, he waited while she sat in the front passenger seat before he reached to grab something from the back. "Here," he said softly, wrapping her in a blanket. "Wait here while I make a phone call." Then he shut the door, and she watched as he pulled out his cell phone and dialed someone.

Aware of the pleasant scent inside his vehicle, she tightened the blanket around her. She watched as Elijah skirted his car and got in on the driver's side.

"I called Jacob. He'll be here soon. He'll check to be sure your horse is all right, then drive your buggy home. We'll follow him in my car." He turned to study her carefully. "I should take you to the hospital to have you looked at. You have a nasty bump around the scrape."

"I'll be all right," she assured him. "I'll have my mother look at it when I get home." She remembered the phone that she had to find. She hadn't been thinking clearly when she got out. She was upset that she hadn't looked for the phone to call for help. Thankfully, Elijah had arrived when he did. "I think my cell phone fell on the floor of the buggy. I had it on the seat beside me before the accident."

Elijah scowled. "A driver ran you off the road and kept going. That was no accident but someone's stupidity in racing instead of slowing down in the snow."

Mary gazed at him, happy he was there and that he'd cared enough to make sure she got home safely. She was grateful for his kindness and his rescue. She wanted to tell him so, but before she could, she saw headlights approaching them from behind.

"Here's Jacob now," Elijah told Mary as a car pulled off the road behind his vehicle. He climbed out as Jacob walked over. "Thanks for coming, brother."

"Is she okay?" Jacob asked.

"Hit her head. She was freezing when I found her. Shaking all over. She told me she felt dizzy when she tried to get back inside." He met Jacob's gaze. "I'm worried about her.

The trembling is more about what happened than the cold, I think." Elijah gestured toward her buggy. "Would you check on her mare and be sure she's not injured? The buggy seems all right, but if you'll take another look, I'd appreciate it."

His brother nodded. "Will do. Give me a few minutes."

"Great. We'll follow you to the Troyer home after." Elijah glanced toward the car, noting Mary huddled in his blanket in the dashboard light. "Oh, and she thinks her cell phone fell on the floor when her vehicle bumped through the ditch and onto the field."

Jacob nodded. "I'll get it for her."

Elijah watched Jacob go to the horse first. He could care for horses and other livestock, but his brother was the best one to give aid to Mary's horse since he was an equine veterinarian. Unlike him, Jacob had chosen to work in a larger practice.

Elijah got into his car. "Jacob is checking your mare. Horses are his specialty. I can care for horses and large farm animals if no one else is available, but I'm a small animal veterinarian. Jacob is the one you need right now." He paused to study her. She still appeared a bit shaken up. "Are you warm enough? Or do you want me to crank up the heat?"

"I'm fine," Mary assured him. "What will I do if my horse is injured or my buggy's damaged?"

"Not to worry, we'll figure it out." Mary closed her eyes and nodded. As he studied her pallor, he grew concerned. His heart had nearly leapt out of his chest when he'd found her hurt and frightened on the side of the road. What would have happened if he hadn't been here to help her? If he'd assumed she'd made it home safely...or someone else had come along and taken advantage of her vulnerability? He became upset by the mere thought of her stuck in the snow for hours, injured and freezing. As he continued to make sure she was all right, he saw that she looked pale and worried. "Mary, are you okay?"

She opened her eyes again. "Thanks to you."

"Night is dangerous for your buggies on the road," he said softly. "I'm glad we agreed to change your hours. Traveling by daylight is safer. But the next time it snows? Stay home. Okay?"

She hesitated before she nodded. "But who will work reception or do the books if I'm not there?"

"First, if it's snowing, many of our clients will cancel unless it's something serious." He offered her a soft smile. "It'll be fine. I'll make do. I can close the office if there is a storm. New Berne Animal Hospital should be able to handle emergencies."

"But—"

"No *buts*, Mary," he said. "It's not worth risking your life to get into the office on a snowy or icy road." He saw his brother heading in their direction. Jacob approached his side of the car, and Elijah got out of his car, quickly closing the door to keep the heat inside. "Well?"

"The mare seems fine," Jacob told him. "Like you, I couldn't find anything wrong with her buggy. I found this on the floor." He handed Elijah Mary's flip phone.

"Thanks, Jacob," Elijah said. "So, you're confident that you can drive her buggy safely home for her?"

His brother nodded. "Ask her for her address, and I'll get directions on my phone." Jacob looked toward his vehicle. "Think it will be okay to leave my car here?"

Elijah nodded. "It's far enough off the road yet away from the ditch. I'll bring you back as soon as we get Mary and her buggy home."

"I'm going to walk the horse carefully through the ditch. There is a place just up ahead where it will be easier to get her buggy back onto the road." Elijah peered into the darkness and saw the gradual slope his brother was referring to. He'd be able to get back on the pavement from there. Jacob left his side and went to Mary's buggy.

Elijah got back into his car and handed Mary her cell phone.

"Thank you," she said, sounding grateful. He saw her face illuminated in the interior car light as she blinked back tears.

"You're welcome." He resisted the urge to wrap his arm around her, which would be inappropriate since he was her boss. He felt drawn to her but refused to give in to the attraction although he was aware of it every time he was in her company. "What's your address?" he asked, and she gave it to him.

Jacob came back after leading the buggy closer to the road and Elijah put down the window again. "I'm going to need your help getting her horse and buggy onto the road."

"You steer," Elijah said, getting out of the car.

She gazed at him with a worried look as he turned to close the door. "Please don't hurt yourself on my account."

"We'll be careful," he told her before he left her and strode toward his brother, who had already climbed into the buggy on the driver's side. Elijah gave him Mary's address and waited while Jacob put it into his phone. "I think I know where that property is," he said. "Ready to get this back on the road?"

Elijah nodded, and his brother flicked the leathers, urging the horse on. Elijah carefully walked to the rear of the buggy and pushed, which made moving it forward easier. He slipped once, but after the initial push, he found his footing again as the buggy moved without help until it was back on the road. With a nod at Jacob, he returned to his car.

"It's all right," he said to Mary.

Mary looked relieved. "Thank you for everything you've done."

He smiled. "I have to take care of my best employee." And was glad to see her small smile.

The snow continued to fall, and Elijah followed Jacob, who drove slowly and carefully.

"There!" Mary cried as she gestured toward a driveway that, in the dim light, Elijah saw led to a two-story farmhouse.

Jacob made the turn, and Elijah drove in behind him. His brother steered toward the barn and parked before he got out and approached Elijah's car. Elijah parked as well and rolled down the window for his brother. "Mary, do you want me to unhitch the horse and settle it and your buggy in the barn?"

She blinked. "Can you do that?"

"Yes," he said and then grinned.

"That would be *wunderbor*," she replied, and Elijah noticed her use of Pennsylvania *Deitsch*.

Elijah stayed in the car while Jacob handled the horse and Mary's vehicle. When he was done in the barn, Jacob returned, bending his head to better see her as Elijah rolled down the window. "All set, Mary."

He heard her sniff.

"Do you want me to walk you to your door?" Elijah asked.

"*Nay*, I'll be fine." She glanced at his brother, who opened the car door for her. "Thank you, Jacob." She climbed out with help.

"You'd best get your head looked after," Jacob said.

Mary skirted the car. "Oh, your blanket," she said to Elijah as she started to unwrap it.

"Keep it. I'm glad I had it for you to use." Mary swayed after taking only a few steps toward the house. Elijah got out of the car in a hurry. "Mary!" he called as he turned on his phone flashlight. She stopped and faced him. "You're not feeling well. *Please* let me walk you to your door." When she didn't object this time, he gently slipped his arm around her waist and walked her slowly toward the house. The last thing he wanted was for her to trip and fall on the snow. Once they reached the side door, he opened the screen for her, eager to see her inside and escape. He was nervous about being on property belonging to her Amish family, but he'd walk her inside if she needed him. "Will you be all right?"

"Yes, thank you," she murmured, her gaze filled with gratitude.

"Keep your cell phone close. I'll call you later tonight to see how you are doing. Looks like the snow won't be stopping anytime soon. The office will be closed tomorrow." Once Mary was inside the house, he returned to his vehicle, where Jacob sat in the front passenger seat.

"Let's get you back to your SUV," he said, turning to face his brother. "Thank you for your help."

Eyeing him, Jacob wore a funny smile. "You like her."

Elijah frowned. "She's my employee. Of course, I like her."

"Maybe," his brother said.

Ignoring him, Elijah put the car in gear and drove down the lane away from the Troyer property. He refused to let Jacob goad him. Mary was a capable woman. Why wouldn't he like her? That didn't mean he wasn't intrigued by her. So what if he thought her pretty? He would allow nothing more than friendship between them. They had a good working relationship and he wasn't about to allow that to change.

When he finally got home that night after dropping Jacob off, he was tired and hungry. Still, his thoughts centered on Mary and how her vulnerability tugged at him. She was his employee, as he'd told his older brother. Then why couldn't he put her out of his mind?

* * *

"Mary, you're late," her mother said as Mary opened the outside door and entered the kitchen. "Although it hasn't been snowing long, I figured you'd have to go slow on the road."

"I know," she said, still shaken by the accident.

Mam glanced at her and frowned, her gaze taking in her facial injury, the snow on her head and the blanket wrapped around her. Her mother's expression turned tight with worry. "Something happened. What?"

Still shaken by the experience, Mary swallowed hard before answering. "Had an accident. A car that passed me was traveling too fast."

"Are you *oll recht*?" Her *mam* approached and examined her forehead.

Mary nodded. "I am now. I got out of the buggy to check on the horse, but then I couldn't get back inside." At her mother's growing look of concern, she continued. "Someone stopped to help me."

"*Dochter,* you're home safe and sound, so whoever came to your aid must be a *gut* person." Mam went to get a bag of ice from the freezer and returned to place it against the bump on Mary's forehead. "Hold this here and sit down. You must be cold. Would you like a cup of tea to warm you?"

"*Ja*, please." She was cold, and the ice on her head wasn't helping her condition.

After she placed tea before her daughter, her mother sat down in the chair next to her. "Tell me about this Good Samaritan. He gave you the blanket?"

Mary nodded as she put the bag of ice on the table so she could drink her tea and cradle her cup. "He did, and he wasn't a stranger. Dr. Zook was the one who found me. When he saw it was snowing, he decided to follow me to make sure I got here safely. I was so cold and couldn't get back into the buggy to find my phone to call for help. I thank the Lord that he came when he did. He helped me into his car and gave me the blanket so I could get warm."

Her mother nodded, looking relieved. "That was kind of him," she commented. "So, he checked everything out before he allowed you to drive home?"

"*Nay*, he called his brother who is also a veterinarian to help. Jacob examined our horse and then drove our buggy home for me while Dr. Zook followed him with me in his car." Mary took another sip of hot tea. "When we got here, Dr. Zook insisted on walking me to the *haus*, although I told him I was fine. Then he and his brother left so Jacob could get back to his car."

Her father entered the room. He frowned when he saw her face. "What happened?" he asked, and her mother explained. "One more reason why you shouldn't be out on the road at dark, *dochter*," her father said upon hearing the story. "Did you ask him to change your hours yet?"

"*Nay*, he's the one who mentioned it first today, actually— and that was before I left and saw the change in the weather. He also told me that from now on, I wasn't to come into the office or drive home when the roads are snowy or icy."

Dat's gaze softened. "That's the sign of a *gut* man. I'm glad he was concerned enough to check on you."

"Me, too," Mary murmured. She finished the last swallow of tea. "So, what can I do to help with supper?" She started to rise.

Mam waved at her to stay seated. "There is nothing to do. I knew you'd be later than usual after I saw it was snowing, so I decided on chicken corn chowder and sandwiches."

"Sounds *wunderbor*," Mary said.

"Are you warm enough now?" Mam asked.

She smiled at her mother. "*Ja*."

Her mam rose to turn on the burner and set down the pan of soup that she'd pulled from the refrigerator. "*Gut.* Put that ice pack back on. I'll check the swelling later to see if it has gone down any."

Her *dat* stood and approached his wife. "What can I do to help?"

Mam shook her head. "Tell Simeon that supper will be ready soon and perhaps find out what he'd like to drink."

Mary felt much better in the warmth of their family home where their gas stove gave off enough heat to fill the kitchen and beyond. She was grateful for her parents who loved her... and her brother who might tease her at times but whom she loved all the same. Then she thought of her older brother David, now married to his sweetheart and Mary's friend, Fannie Miller Troyer.

She felt truly blessed...not only for her loved ones but for the goodness Elijah showed her more each day and proof that she was valued in the office. As per his instructions, Mary kept her cell phone close. He said he'd call and check in with her, and grateful for his concern she believed him. Her boss was so much more than she'd ever expected. She wondered now why she'd been nervous to work with him while Beatrice was absent. He was a handsome man, who often made her stomach flutter with butterflies and her heart race whenever she spent time with him. And since rescuing her on the side of the road, he'd become more than her employer in her eyes. He was a hero who'd saved her from fear and the cold.

Her phone was charged as she plugged it in each day near her desk. She'd made sure her battery pack was full as well, enough to last the weekend, especially since it was mostly for emergency use or to call into work when she was sick. But she'd not missed a single day of work, except for one day that Beatrice had given her off to attend David and Fannie's wedding.

Supper was easy, and it didn't take long to enjoy it. Mary insisted on helping her mother clean up, but her father told her she should rest after her ordeal.

She hoped Elijah would check on her before bedtime. She was grateful for his help and his kindness even though she knew she liked her employer and boss way more than she should for an Englisher. Even if he felt the same way, she could never have a future with him. She hadn't joined the church yet, but she enjoyed her life in the Amish community too much to give it up. And for some reason, she knew that he preferred the English life he lived, working as a veterinarian. Things could never be what she wanted. Mary sighed. She would just have to keep reminding herself that someday she'd find an Amish man to settle down with and raise a family. But at this moment, she couldn't take comfort from it...for she still cared more for Elijah than any of the young men who had taken her home from singings when she was younger. And that was a big problem for her.

Mary went upstairs to her room and sat awhile to see whether the snow had stopped and waited...until it was late, when she knew he wasn't going to call her tonight.

She sighed, more than a little disappointed. And then her phone rang.

Chapter Nine

Mary quickly answered the call. "Hello?"

"Mary, I'm sorry to be calling so late." She was relieved when she finally heard Elijah's deep voice on the line. "How are you? How's your head?"

Her heart warmed. "It's fine. Mam gave me an ice pack for it. I didn't keep it on long since I was still cold, but then I used it after I drank hot tea." The ice pack had eased the sting of her scrape and the swelling around it.

"That's good." He paused. "Were your parents upset to learn what happened?"

"Yes, but they were glad you stopped to help me." She waited for him to say something, and when he didn't, she added, "The other day my father told me to ask you for a change in my hours, but you insisted before I could say anything. I appreciate it." Uncomfortable and feeling suddenly shy after what she'd just confessed, she blurted out, "Will you thank Jacob for me? It was nice of him to come out and help." Although she had to silently admit that she'd been happier when she'd recognized Elijah climbing out of his car earlier to come to her aid.

"Did you take Tylenol for your headache?" he teased.

She knew he was referencing her advice from the day before and laughed. "No, my mother has other remedies for pain." Including using a fragrant oil to rub away the ache.

"Tylenol does help," he told her.

Mary agreed, but the Old Order Amish used other methods first before resorting to English painkillers. For convenience's sake, she used Tylenol whenever she needed to alleviate pain in the office. Every church district had different rules, and she was grateful that the harsh rules like those belonging to the more strict communities didn't apply to theirs. "Did you have any trouble getting home?" she asked. The last time she'd looked, the snow was still coming down.

"I drove slowly, so I made the trip without incident," he said. "I called Jacob to make sure he made it home safely, too. He did. I didn't think he'd have a problem since his vehicle has four-wheel drive."

She didn't know what four-wheel drive meant, but she thought it must be a good thing if the car drove more easily over the snow-covered road.

"I called a radio station to announce the closing of our office, and the weather forecast is grim with more," Elijah told her. "I'm glad I made the decision to close earlier."

"The roads are bad." Mary bit her lip. Her mind on work now, she asked, "Did you see the résumés I left on your desk this morning?"

"I saw them but decided they can wait until next week, especially since Jacob has promised me vet tech help the three days before the holiday and the week after." He grew quiet but didn't seem to be in a hurry to end the call. "If the roads haven't improved by Monday, you should stay home, even if we're open. But if you decide you want to work, I'd prefer to take you to and from the office. I'll keep an eye on the weather forecast and check our answering service tomorrow to see if any clients have already called to cancel their appointments. No sense heading in if there are no patients."

"True." Now that they were getting along well, Mary

wanted to work on Monday. She grew quiet, unsure how to continue their conversation. She wasn't ready to hang up. She loved hearing the sound of his voice and the way he spoke to her made her feel as if she was important to the office. Because of it, she felt warm and tingly inside…and eager to see him again.

Elijah hesitated, but before she could think of what to say, he spoke. "I best let you go so you can get some rest."

Mary nodded, although she knew he couldn't see her. "Thank you for calling, Elijah, and for saving me today."

"I'm glad I found you," he confessed. "It scares me to think that someone unsavory might have stopped instead of me. Good night, Mary. Take care of yourself. We have a long weekend now, so rest up."

She smiled. "Good night. Rest up as well. You've been working too hard and deserve the break."

"I don't know about that," he said, "but I'll rest anyway. Bye, Mary."

He hung up before she could whisper, "Bye, Elijah."

The snow stopped during the night, but the next morning, the temperatures remained well below freezing. Seated at his kitchen table, Elijah gazed into his side yard and watched as a cardinal flew from one tree branch to another. After a good night's sleep, he was in no hurry to do anything but laze around the house. He'd called his answering service last night to change the message to include the clinic's closure today. His thoughts turned to Mary. He wondered how she was faring and promised himself that he'd call her later when he was sure she'd be awake. He couldn't help his concern for her.

Seeing her frightened, pale face after her accident yesterday had shaken him. He couldn't get her out of his mind. She was a good woman and an excellent employee. He was finally getting to know her better, and he liked what he'd discovered.

The weather forecast called for a sunny but frigid day. The snow wouldn't be melting anytime soon, and news reports claimed the roads would still be too dangerous to drive on tomorrow and over the weekend.

Elijah enjoyed a cup of coffee and a bowl of cornflakes with milk. When he was done, he looked at the time and dialed Mary's cell number.

"*Hallo?*" a male voice said.

"I...is Mary there?" Had he dialed the wrong number? "This is her phone, isn't it?"

"*Ja*, she left it on the table," the man said. "I'll get her. One moment, please."

The line went silent, and then Mary's sweet voice came on the line. "This is Mary."

"Hey. It's Elijah," he ventured. "Was that your brother?"

"Yes, Simeon, the younger one."

"I thought I'd had the wrong number when he answered," he told her. "I'm just checking in. How are you feeling?"

"I'm doing much better," she replied. "Thanks to you."

He smiled, pleased to know that she was faring well and felt grateful. "No headache?"

"Not since I started drinking a special herbal tea my mother made for me," Mary said, and he could hear the good humor in her answer. "Maybe I should bring some in for you to try."

Elijah shuddered. "Ah... I like coffee more than tea. And caffeine helps headaches, too, right? As long as the headache isn't due to too much of it."

"*Ja*, I heard something about that." She paused. "What are you doing?" she asked, much to his surprise.

"Bird-watching through my kitchen window." He took

a quick sip of coffee. "I have cardinals in my yard. They're beautiful and my favorite."

"Oh, yes!" Mary's tone told him she felt the same way.

"What are you doing on this bright Thursday morning?" The moment the words were out of his mouth, he wondered why he was asking. This conversation was moving past employer-employee territory. Although he liked her, it wasn't as if he could ever have a relationship with her. She was Amish, and he was English and a shunned member of his former Amish community. He had to remind himself that he and Mary were never going to be more than friends. They shouldn't be anything but colleagues...

"I'm tidying my room." She laughed. "Although my *mam* wants me to rest today."

"Hmm" was his only answer. "Seems like there is a better use for your time."

Her laughter was rich. "You want something to eat on Monday?"

He had to think for a moment before he spoke. "Always."

"With the weather keeping us in tomorrow, Mam and I plan to do the baking tomorrow instead of Saturday," she said, and he could practically see the smile on her face.

He grew silent. "Mary, will you come to work if we open on Monday? You don't have to decide now," he added quickly.

"If you'll be in the clinic," she said, "then yes, I want to work."

"I'll pick you up, then. Even if the snow has melted by Monday, you suffered a traumatic experience, and I'd feel better if I drove you." He felt an increase in his heartbeat as he waited for her response. Elijah wanted nothing more than to drive to work with her seated in his car next to him, but he was afraid his offer had made her uncomfortable.

"Okay," she said softly.

"Good." He smiled, more than a little pleased. "Do you happen to recall anyone who was on today's schedule that I need to call?"

"I do," she admitted. "It's a light day."

Elijah was relieved. "Good. I wish I'd thought to bring a print copy home with me."

"Let me think a minute," she said softly. Then she rattled off the names of the patients on today's schedule. "I hope I haven't missed anyone."

"Thanks, Mary. I'll use my phone to log into the system and check. I want to get their contact information so I call them about the cancellation and ask that they call back to reschedule." Talking with her gave him a rush of pleasure, and he didn't know why. "I'll let you go. Please take care of yourself. Listen to your mother and rest."

"I will," she murmured. "Enjoy your long weekend."

He hung up the phone and set it next to him on his kitchen table. It rang a few seconds later. He glanced at the caller ID. "Jacob," he said when he connected.

"I'm on my way to Mary's," his brother informed him by way of greeting. "I want to check on her mare to make sure she's all right. Would you give her a call and let her know? I don't want anyone in her family to worry when I drive onto their property. I'll let them know I'm here before I head into their barn."

He was unsure how he felt about his brother heading to Mary's house, although he knew Jacob wouldn't do anything to upset her. But Jacob was right that her mare needed to be looked at again in daylight. "I'll call."

"Great. Thanks," Jacob said. "I'll let you know how I make out."

Elijah dialed Mary's phone again. "Hi," he said when she answered. "It's me again. I just heard from Jacob. He's on his way to examine your horse. He'll let you know when he's there. Please tell your father and mother that he isn't there to steal from your family," he joked. "He just wants to make sure that there are no aftereffects to your mare since last night's accident."

"Oh," she breathed. "I'll tell them. Thank you for letting me know."

"You're welcome," he said. "I'll call you later about work on Monday." After a brief goodbye, Elijah hung up the phone and got up to do a few things he'd put off doing, like cleaning his place and doing laundry. He fought back the urge to talk with Mary again and needed something to keep him busy.

He waited for Jacob to call him with an update that Mary's horse was okay.

"That's Dr. Zook's *bruder*?" her father asked as Jacob pulled his car close to the barn and got out later that morning.

"*Ja*, he's a veterinarian, too," Mary said as she watched him through the window as he approached the house and knocked. "His specialty is horses."

"Hmm," Dat said before he opened the door.

"Hello," Jacob greeted. "I'm here to check on Bess after yesterday's accident."

"*Gut* of you to come," her father replied. "You know where the mare is?"

Mary didn't hear Jacob and realized that he must have nodded.

"What are you doing?" she asked with alarm when Dat reached for his coat and put it on. "Going to talk with the man." He grabbed his hat and settled it on his head.

"Why?" Mary dared to inquire.

His father stopped, his hand on the doorknob, and looked

at her. He frowned. "I need to know how much I'll have to pay for his services."

She blinked. "*Ach. Gut* idea." Then she watched as he left the house and strode to the barn where the man inside was examining Bess.

Feeling the sudden need to be there as well, Mary pulled on her black woolen cloak before hurrying out into the cold toward the barn. She entered the outbuilding and found Jacob in Bess's stall with her father observing Jacob's examination.

Her *dat* murmured something she couldn't hear, and Jacob laughed, causing Mary to relax. The man had been kind to her, and she didn't want there to be any discord between Elijah's brother and her family.

"*Vadder*," Mary said as she approached. "How is Bess?" She joined him outside the stall.

"Mary." Jacob looked over and met her gaze from where he held a stethoscope against the mare's left chest area below the elbow. He shifted the stethoscope to the horse's abdomen before moving to the animal's chest area on its right side. "Her vitals are good despite her trauma. I don't see anything to worry about, but if something changes, just reach out to Elijah, and he'll immediately get in touch with me."

"*Danki*," her father said. "I appreciate the visit. How much do I owe you?"

"Nothing," Jacob assured him with a small smile. "I won't take your money. Your daughter is my brother's employee and a hard worker, according to him. I'm just glad we were able to help her." He rose to his feet. "You know, I know a little about buggies and wagons from my Amish clients. Shall we take a look at yours?"

Her *dat* nodded. "Would appreciate it. You didn't have any trouble driving it here?"

"Not a bit," Jacob said. "Your buggy didn't look damaged

in the dark, but it's best if we take another look." His blue gaze, so much like Elijah's, settled on Mary. "You okay? Not worse for wear after last night?"

"Yes and no, thanks." Chilled by the memory, Mary wrapped her arms around herself.

"*Dochter*," Dat said, "go inside where it's warm. I'm sure your *mam* will be waiting on you. I doubt your boss will appreciate you getting sick."

She nodded, knowing he was right. "Thank you, Jacob."

He grinned. "It's what I do." Jacob addressed her father, "Let's take a look at your vehicle."

Mary left, relieved by her parent's acceptance of Jacob's visit and the news that Bess was all right.

When Mary entered the house, her mother was in the kitchen. "Ah, there you are, *dochter*! Where have you been?"

"Outside with Dat and Jacob. Bess is fine. They are checking for damage to our buggy." Even though Jacob had been able to get it here safely, Mary prayed that it was fine since while the wheels were all right, it was hard to fully tell if the body sustained damage. Last evening had been a frightening experience for her. She was grateful that Elijah had insisted on driving her to work and back on Monday, as she wasn't ready to be in a buggy on the road alone. Although, while she was happy to ride with Elijah, she didn't know how her parents would feel about her riding unchaperoned with her employer.

Mary sighed. It shouldn't be a problem, she thought. They already knew that she and Elijah worked alone in the clinic together although there were constantly health visits from clients and their pets. Besides, in her parents' eyes, her boss was the man who had saved her and took her home after the accident.

Please, Lord, I want to go to work. My family has a lot to be thankful for when it comes to the Zook brothers. As do I.

"Let's have some tea," Mam said.

Mary hid her concern with a smile. "*Okey.*"

"Would you like some jelly bread?" her mother asked.

"Sounds *gut.*" Mary rose to take out the jelly until her *mam* gave her a look that made her sit down again.

Mary wondered if she'd hear from Elijah again today or if she would have to wait until tomorrow. She'd spoken with him twice now, so she shouldn't be disappointed if he didn't call again. But she wanted to hear from him anyway.

Chapter Ten

Elijah drove Mary to work Monday morning.

"Thanks for picking me up," Mary said softly as she got in the car.

"The roads are mainly cleared," he replied as he put on his blinker and made a turn. "But I still feel better taking you. It's not safe for a buggy yet. There are too many crazy people who drive too fast."

"Another accident waiting to happen." She shuddered, tightening her cloak around her to get warm.

He glanced at her and frowned. "Are you all right? You're not afraid of riding in my car, are you?"

"No, not at all." She shifted in her seat so she could better see through the windshield. Mary felt relaxed with him at the wheel. "Just remembering the accident."

He eyed her with concern. "I've been unable to forget it."

She met his gaze. "Me either," she whispered. "Jacob said there wasn't any damage to our buggy—I realize that the jolt I felt when I bumped my head was because the car spooked my mare Bess, causing her to rear up before she bolted into the field."

"He told me the same thing, but that doesn't mean you couldn't have been seriously hurt." She saw his hands tightening on the steering wheel. "Your buggy could have rolled over with you trapped inside."

"I know." She shuddered at the memory. "At least, we know the horse and buggy are fine."

He nodded as he looked at her briefly. "Yes, that's good."

Elijah drove competently, and she felt safe with him. His scent filled the car, a blend of soap, something else pleasing to her nose, and a unique male fragrance that she'd recognized early on as belonging only to him.

He signaled and turned into the clinic entrance. Elijah parked close to the back of the building, then got out, came around to her side, and opened her door for her. Surprised by his actions, she gave him a shy smile and took the hand he extended to her, then climbed out with his assistance.

"Thank you," she said, "but the baked goods I brought are on the back seat."

He grinned. "I know. Let me get you inside, then I'll go back for them."

The building's heat was set to automatically turn on early in the morning. Mary felt nice and warm as she hung up her cloak. Elijah entered moments later with her container of muffins and thick slices of homemade bread.

"I don't know what's in here, but whatever it is, it smells amazing," he announced as he handed the baking to her before he removed his coat and took off his navy woolen cap, stuffing it in his jacket sleeve before storing it in the walk-in closet.

"I'll make coffee," she announced as she carried the container to the table in the break room before setting up the coffeepot to brew.

Mary then went to her desk and turned on her computer. After opening the clinic, she walked by the side window, pausing to enjoy the view of the glistening snow-covered lawn in the morning sun. Especially since they'd arrived without incident, thanks to Elijah.

She checked the schedule and the answering machine, pleased to note that no one else had called to cancel their appointments. The front door opened, and a young woman entered the building.

"Hi, I'm Lacey Jones," she said with a smile. "Jacob asked me to come and help his brother today."

Mary gazed at the young woman, noting how pretty she was with her dark brown hair, large brown eyes and bright smile. She rose and beamed at her. "Hi, Lacey. Welcome! Come with me, and I'll take you to him."

"Thanks," Lacey murmured and followed Mary to Elijah's office, where she introduced her boss to the new temporary assistant.

Elijah was happy with his full schedule, the knowledge that Mary was safely at the front desk and the help his brother had sent them in the form of Lacey Jones, who'd arrived on time as promised. The day went by quickly. Mary handled the front area efficiently, and Lacey performed her job well just as his brother had promised. And Jacob would know since she'd been a vet tech at New Berne Animal Hospital for several months now.

Elijah decided to order sandwiches for delivery at lunchtime, and the women were appreciative. They all took a moment to enjoy their food and then went back to work. Just as Mary had predicted, the schedule was packed with rescheduled clients wanting their pets to be seen before the holiday weekend coming up. And the hours left in the day simply flew by until all patients were seen.

"Good night, Dr. Zook," Lacey said politely after he'd told her she could leave for the day. "Have a nice night!"

"Will you be back tomorrow?" he asked, hoping she'd say

yes since she was a great worker who kept up easily with the busy schedule.

"I'll be back tomorrow, but I can't make it on Wednesday," she said. "Georgie will be here to cover for me while I'm away. My family is leaving for New Jersey to spend the Thanksgiving holiday weekend with my grandparents and my dad's siblings and my cousins."

Elijah smiled at her. "Thank you for a great job, Lacey. I'll see you tomorrow. I'm going to call my brother and let him know how well you did today."

The woman smiled, appearing pleased, and then left.

It was getting late. He went to the front desk to check on Mary. "Everything all right?" he asked.

"All good," she said, her blue eyes mirroring her satisfaction as she met his gaze. "I just need a few minutes to add today's receipts to Beatrice's bookkeeping program." She leaned back in her chair. "Do you want to leave now?"

He shook his head. "When you're ready, let me know. There is some work I can do in my office." He gave her a wry smile. "I still have to go over those résumés you gave me the other day." She beamed at him, and he couldn't look away… until he forced himself to go to his office.

But once at his desk, Elijah couldn't concentrate, lacking the energy to read the résumés in-depth. He'd go over them another day. He poured himself coffee and brought it back to his desk to sip on while he waited for Mary to tell him she was done.

He longed to spend more time with her outside the clinic. If he drove her home slowly, he could extend his time with her. And while they couldn't be sweethearts, he figured there would be nothing wrong with taking a friend out for a meal. At least he hoped.

* * *

It was closing time and she hadn't locked the front door yet. When someone came in. Mary looked up, blinked and then stared when she saw her father, wearing a navy woolen jacket and black-banded straw hat, enter the waiting room. He approached her desk with a small puppy in his arms.

"Dat," she gasped, "what are you doing here?"

"I brought this little dog in to see Dr. Zook," he said. "Simeon found him on the side of the road, curled up in a ball in the snow without his mother or siblings. He needs care as he's been shaking hard ever since your *bruder* brought him into the *haus*. I fear he is ill."

Mary studied the dog in her father's arms. He was a bundle of white fur with patches of tan here and there with dark eye and a pink and black nose. She could see he was trembling all over, even tucked up against the warmth of her *dat*'s coat. "Poor thing," she murmured. "He also looks half-starved. He does need to be seen to. Thanks for bringing him in. I'll tell Dr. Zook that you're here."

Her father nodded. "Simeon wants to keep him," he told her as she stood.

"Will you let him?" she asked. If it hadn't been for the condition of the puppy, Mary would have wondered whether her father would have used the little dog as an excuse to meet her employer.

"He does grow on you," he replied, his voice soft. "A friend wanted to give me a dog when I was little, but my *vadder* wouldn't let me have it."

Her heart melted a little. Mary had always known that her parents were different than others within the community who made it a priority to care for their horses and livestock like her family did. But pets, like dogs and cats? Small animals held no value for most Amish families, so it was rare to see someone within the community like her *dat* who cared about them.

She smiled at him, touched by his concern for a little stray dog. "I'll be right back. Please feel free to take a seat while you wait."

Mary found Elijah in his office. "I know it's late, and you're probably ready to go home. But will you have time to see one more patient? Someone is here with a puppy that needs to be seen. The dog was found in the snow on the side of the road, shivering."

Dr. Zook looked concerned. "I'd never turn away an animal who needs care," he said.

"Thank you," she responded, grateful for his compassion and work ethic. "Ah, before I bring him to an exam room, I must warn you that the man is my father. My brother Simeon found the puppy on the side of the road. The dog doesn't have a collar."

"I'll be happy to see them. He came at the right time." She watched as Elijah shifted some papers into a file folder. "So, the man is your father," he said.

Mary cast him a worried look. "*Ja*," she replied, unaware that she'd slipped into Pennsylvania *Deitsch* until the word came out of her mouth.

"Take him to exam room two, and I'll be right in." She stood there long enough to see Elijah open his top desk drawer and slide the folder inside.

Mary left then, hurrying to see her father, who remained standing by the reception window, cradling the puppy in his big arms. "Dat, Dr. Zook is glad you came in when you did. Would you please follow me?" She was aware of her father behind her as she led him down the hall to the exam room. "Dr. Zook will be right in."

Once inside, she gestured toward a chair. "It's *okey* to have a seat." As she turned to leave, she saw Elijah in the doorway.

"Mr. Troyer?" Elijah greeted. "I'm Dr. Zook. Mary tells me you have a sick puppy."

The man nodded. "Please call me Samuel."

"Samuel." Elijah smiled, then studied the dog in her father's arms. Mary stood outside the open doorway. This was her *dat*, and she worried he'd ask her boss personal or embarrassing questions to take Elijah's measure on how he liked working with his daughter.

She saw Elijah eyeing the dog. "May I take him?" he asked her father.

Her *dat* carefully handed Elijah the puppy.

Elijah saw Mary standing in the open doorway. "I've got this," he said, not unkindly.

Mary felt her face heat as she nodded, then left. She only hoped her father hadn't noticed her attraction to Dr. Zook.

She tried to think about the two men in the exam room as she returned to her desk to finish her bookkeeping for the day. It seemed to take forever for the puppy's exam, but she stifled the urge to check on her father and Elijah. She found small comfort in the knowledge that her *dat* had liked Jacob. Maybe he'd like Elijah as well, especially knowing he'd been her rescuer on that dark, snowy, terrifying night last week.

Her father entered the reception area with the puppy curled inside a cardboard box, wrapped in a blue blanket she recognized as one of those Elijah kept in stock to keep a patient warm for emergencies such as this one. "I was going to suggest I bring you home, but Dr. Zook said you have a little more work to finish and that he'd take you."

Mary nodded, glad that Elijah had offered to drive her. She felt safe riding with him in his car. She wasn't eagerly ready to be in a buggy again. "How is he?" she asked, gesturing toward the puppy.

Her *dat* smiled. "He's doing well, considering. Dr. Zook suggested a brand of food that's good for him, but first, he wants us to feed him boiled chicken breast and rice for a few days so that he doesn't get sick to his stomach after not eating. He also gave me an antibiotic for him." He glanced at the sleeping dog with a soft look. "He wants to see him again after Thanksgiving. Would you make an appointment?"

"Of course." She checked the schedule for the week after the holiday. "Any specific day?"

"Either Monday or Tuesday," Dat said as he rubbed a finger across the puppy's white head. "Simeon has those two days off, and I know he'll want to bring this little guy in for his visit."

Mary looked up from her computer. "There is an opening on Tuesday afternoon at two. Will that work?"

Her father nodded, and Mary added the appointment to the schedule.

"All set," she said with a smile. She leaned closer for another look at the puppy. "He is adorable." Mary met her father's gaze. "Did you or Simeon name him yet?"

"Not yet, but I'm sure we'll be talking about it once I get home," he replied. "Dr. Zook—Elijah—refuses to charge me because you work for him." He grinned. "I've convinced him to come for a meal sometime next week as a thank you. I told him the two of you can discuss when."

Mary hid her shock. She was surprised that Elijah had finally consented to eat with her family. "*Ach, gut,*" she murmured. She was secretly pleased but worried at the same time about him meeting her family.

"I'll see you at home, *dochter,*" he said as he headed toward the door. "Mam has already started supper. Baked chicken with scalloped potatoes and sweet-and-sour chowchow."

"Sounds delicious." Mary watched him open the door, but before he could close it behind him, she said, "Be careful going home, Dat." His answer was a smile and a nod, meant to reassure her.

Mary quickly entered the last of the day's receipts into her laptop.

An hour later, Elijah appeared in her area. "Are you ready to leave? The data entries can wait until tomorrow."

She nodded and turned off the computer. Mary shut off the lights and then followed Elijah to grab their coats. They got ready for the cold silently. She watched as he pulled his woolen hat out of his sleeve, tugging it on until it covered his ears as she slipped on her cloak before they left the building.

Outside, Elijah opened the passenger car door for her. "It will be warm soon." Closing it, he skirted his vehicle and got in. The engine roared to life with his press of a button. Soon, heat filtered into the interior from the dashboard. He pressed two other buttons before he grinned as he met her gaze. "Heated seats."

When she felt the heat through her coat, she laughed. "Modern conveniences. We have heat in our buggies but nothing as nice as this!" She found him studying her with curiosity. "What?"

Elijah shook his head before he drove out of the lot and headed toward Mary's home. The drive was a nice one, and Mary realized that they had reached their destination as Elijah made the turn and drove up to the house. They hadn't discussed her father's invitation to dinner, and she wasn't about to bring it up now.

"Thank you for the ride," she said as she opened the door before he could come around to help her.

"You're welcome," he replied. "I'll be here tomorrow morning at the same time as today."

She grinned. "I appreciate it." As he pulled away, she realized how happy and grateful she was for Elijah's support. She'd just spent the whole day with him, and yet she couldn't wait to see him again.

Chapter Eleven

Elijah was pleased with the short workweek before Thanksgiving. He drove Mary to her house on Wednesday afternoon and opened the door for her. When he extended his hand, he felt a wave of warmth when she took it. Everything had gone well during the past three days with help from his temporary tech but most especially with Mary. He accepted her father's supper invitation and while the prospect of being in the midst of her family made him nervous, he looked forward to seeing Mary in her home.

He smiled at her. "Have a wonderful Thanksgiving, Mary."

"The same to you, Elijah. I hope you have a nice time with your family. Please tell Jacob hello for me." She pulled her coat closer around her before she headed toward the house.

"Mary," he called out as she was about to open the door of the house, "I'll pick you up again on Monday, all right?"

She turned to face him. "That would be wonderful, Elijah. Thank you." Then she let herself into the house. Drawn to her more than he should, he realized how much he would miss her during the four days when he wouldn't be able to see her.

Elijah drove out onto the road and headed home. He thought about going back to the office to pick up work to do on Friday or Saturday when the forecast was for snow, and he'd be stuck at home with no place to go. He could watch some television, he guessed, but he rarely found anything that held his interest. He wasn't sure why he bought a TV set—and a high-definition one at that.

He was hungry, but he didn't feel like cooking. Spying an open take-out Chinese restaurant to his right, he stopped and ordered something to tempt and satisfy him. Once on the road again, Elijah thought of the baked goods and all the wonderful food Mary had thoughtfully brought to share at the office over the past few weeks.

He had a quiet night at home with takeout as he often did. Silent times such as this were vastly different from what his life had been like on his childhood farm with warm family dinners and everyone snuggling in front of the fireplace on cold winter days. Lately, he'd missed those times and wished he had a family to go home to.

The next day, he stopped at the clinic before heading to eat dinner with his family as planned. After parking behind the building, he went into the clinic and grabbed the file folder Mary had left for him. He searched for more work to take with him but decided he'd have to be satisfied with the résumés. After a quick look up front, he thought of Mary seated at her desk, concentrating as she worked hard to finish her tasks. The desk was empty now.

He frowned as he noticed a power pack on her desk that she must have forgotten to take with her—something he knew she'd need to charge her phone. On impulse, he decided to drop it off to her on his way to his family's Thanksgiving dinner. He couldn't stay long. Besides, Mary and her mother were likely preparing their holiday feast.

On the drive to the Troyers, thoughts of her father's invitation to dinner next week rang loudly in his mind. He couldn't turn Samuel down, especially after refusing to charge him for the rescued puppy's care. Mary's father had insisted a meal was his family's way of thanking him. He would go for Mary rather than himself, because he'd just been doing his job.

The Troyer farmhouse came into view on his right. As he pulled into the driveway, he noticed two buggies parked next to each other near the barn. Realizing their guests must already be arriving, he felt a pang of guilt for the intrusion. But it would only take him a minute to give Mary the power pack, and then he'd be on his way to spend the day with his mother, father and two brothers.

He knocked on the side door two times, and it opened, revealing a young man who could be Mary's brother. He eyed Elijah suspiciously. "*Ja?*"

"May I speak with Mary?" Elijah asked politely.

The teenager glanced at the power pack in his hand. "I'll see if she's available."

Samuel Troyer appeared behind his son. "Elijah! Good to see you again! Come in, come in!"

"I can't stay. I'm on my way to my parents. Mary forgot this at the office." He held up the power pack. "I thought she might need it over the long weekend."

The older man nodded. "Come in for a quick moment then," Samuel insisted before he addressed his son. "Simeon, this is Mary's boss and the veterinarian who took care of Snowflake."

"You named him," Elijah said softly to the young man, who nodded. "A good choice considering where you found him."

Simeon smiled. "Thank you for making sure he's *oll recht.*" He turned his head and called, "Mary! There is someone here to see you."

Elijah was ushered indoors and into the kitchen. As he entered the space, he froze, feeling like a deer in headlights as he became the focus of too many sets of Amish eyes to count.

"Elijah!" Mary drew his attention as she got up from the table and approached. "What—"

"You forgot this," he said, his attention now centered on her. After feeling uncomfortable in the company of so many strangers, he immediately felt her calming presence.

"*Ach!*" She beamed at him as he handed her the power pack. "Thank you! I didn't realize that I'd forgotten it."

"Thought you'd need to charge your phone." Mary's bright expression made him glad he'd brought it to her.

She studied him a moment, then turned to address the occupants of the table, who hadn't yet started dinner. "Everyone, this is Dr. Elijah Zook, my boss and a skilled veterinarian."

Everyone greeted him with a *hallo* or a nod. A woman got up with a smile and approached him. She came to stand behind Mary. The two looked so much alike that he decided the older one was her mother.

"Dr. Zook," the woman greeted softly. "I'm Joanna, Mary's *mam*. It's nice to finally meet you."

"Nice to meet you, too," he murmured, his gaze shifting from Mrs. Troyer to Mary.

"May I get you something to eat?" Joanna asked, her features filled with warmth. "A piece of pie? Or some cookies?"

Elijah couldn't help smiling at her. "Thank you for the offer, but I need to head out. My family is expecting me."

"I understand," Mary's mother said while Mary stood silently beside her. "Maybe your family would enjoy some cookies. Let me get you a plate to take with you."

"That's nice of you," he began. "But you don't have to share them."

"I want to," Joanna insisted and flashed Mary a grin." She left and bustled at the counter, returning in seconds with a large plate covered in clear plastic wrap, filled with an array of delicious-looking cookies that smelled wonderful.

"I see where Mary gets her talent for baking," he said as he accepted the treats.

Joanna laughed. "I didn't make these. My daughter did. She comes by it more naturally than me. I taught her a few recipes, yet she's created many we've never tasted before, all of them *wunderbor.*"

Elijah grinned. "I can attest to that." He heard Simeon and his father talking nearby in Pennsylvania *Deitsch*, and he was surprised that despite not hearing the language in years, he understood every word.

"Thank you." He smiled at Mary and her mother. "Enjoy Thanksgiving with your family," he said.

He turned to leave, stopping when Joanna said, "We will see you for supper sometime soon."

He glanced toward Mary and found himself nodding. "I look forward to it." Elijah addressed the others within the room. "*Gut daag*," he said, wishing everyone a good day before he left the house. He smiled at the memory of Mary's surprised expression as he got into his car and drove to his parents' house.

Mary was stunned by Elijah's use of the *Deitsch* words for a good day before he'd left. In serving the New Berne community, had he picked up some of the local Amish language?

She'd been glad to see him and grateful that he'd been thoughtful enough to bring her the power pack she'd need to recharge her phone. She kept her phone charged at her desk whenever she was in the office, but the battery would no doubt fail without a way to charge it over the four-day Thanksgiving weekend. She'd been so involved in cooking with her mother from early this morning that, until Elijah came with the charger, she'd never given a thought that she'd left it at the office.

"So that's Dr. Zook," Simeon said. "It was nice of him to not let us pay for Snowflake's exam."

"*Ja*," her brother David chimed in. "That's the sign of a *gut* and kind man."

"We met his brother first," her father commented. "He helped Elijah rescue Mary after she had a buggy accident last week when it snowed."

"*Accident!*" David looked horrified. "Mary was involved in an accident? Are you *oll recht*?"

"*Ja*," Mary assured her brother, "I'm fine and so is our buggy." She smiled. "I met Jacob last week," she admitted as she tried not to notice the curiosity of everyone at the table. "He came over to help Elijah because he needed an assistant. It was Jacob and Elijah who helped me after the accident. Jacob brought the buggy home while Elijah and I followed him in his car."

"A kind man for sure and certain," Preacher Jonas Miller commented. The minister was the father of Fannie, her brother David's wife.

"Why did he come today?" Jonas's wife Alta asked.

"I forgot the battery pack for my cell phone on my desk at work," Mary said, embarrassed that she'd been so careless. "He'd stopped to pick up something from his office and noticed that I'd forgotten it."

"Huh," DJ, one of Fannie's twin brothers, murmured.

"He may be an Englisher, but he seems like a *gut* man, *ja*?" His twin Danny directed his words to Mary, who could only nod.

"Why don't we pray and give thanks to the Lord before we eat," Mary suggested, feeling her blush at the current topic of conversation—Elijah Zook.

"Will you say the blessing, Jonas?" Mary's mother asked.

The preacher inclined his head. "Hands in our laps, heads

bent and eyes down." He waited a heartbeat and led the room-
ful of her family in a Thanksgiving prayer.

Afterward, lively conversation filled the dinner table as
they passed around dishes of fare and began to eat.

Still, despite the noise all around her, Mary couldn't seem
to get her mind off her employer, who was becoming her
friend.

"What's that you have there?" Jacob queried as Elijah
walked into his parents' house with Joanna Troyer's plate
in his hands. He raised his eyebrows. "Are those cookies?"

"They are," he said with a smile. "Homemade." He grinned
at his mother, who was checking the turkey in the oven.
"Hello, Mom."

She straightened. "Good to see you, son." Her gaze fell on
the plate he held. "You brought homemade cookies? Surely
you didn't bake them yourself," she teased.

"You stopped at the bakery yesterday to get those," his
brother Aaron guessed.

Elijah shook his head. "Got them from Mary when I
stopped there on the way."

Jacob eyed him thoughtfully. "You went over to Mary's?"

"I did." He explained why before setting the cookies on
the countertop in the corner.

His father entered the room. He must have heard the tail
end in the conversation about the power pack as he frowned
when he met Elijah's gaze. "Why would your receptionist
need a power pack at home when she could just plug in her
phone?"

Jacob cleared his throat. "She's Old Order Amish, Dad."

"You have an Amish woman working for you?" Aaron
asked with surprise.

Elijah nodded. "Good worker, too. I couldn't ask for a better employee."

"So, she likes working with animals," Mom said as she pulled the turkey out of the oven and set it on the counter on a hot mat to stand before slicing.

"She's not a vet tech," Jacob told her. "She uses a computer to schedule patients and check them in for their appointments." He grinned. "And Elijah likes her."

Dad frowned. "This Amish woman works on a computer?"

Elijah nodded. "She does. She also inputs my notes into the electronic medical chart program I purchased." He pulled out a kitchen chair and sat down. "And she's been handling the bookkeeping for Beatrice, who will be out for months."

"She is allowed to use technology?" Aaron asked from across the table.

"She told me that members of her community are allowed to use computers at their workplaces and those managing businesses," he told him with a smile. "And she has a flip phone for emergencies."

"I don't know," his mother said. "Seems strange the bishop would allow it..."

"The church elders here are much different than the ones we had in Big Valley," he assured her. "Her community doesn't have the restrictions that ours did. Her father was in yesterday with a puppy Mary's brother found in the snow. He saw Mary working on her computer. It didn't seem to bother him." Still, he couldn't help but remember how uncomfortable he was when he'd entered the Troyer home this morning and saw everyone around the table staring at him, the local preacher and his wife among them. It wasn't until he'd laid eyes on Mary that he'd been able to relax.

"Is it wise to employ a member of the Amish community?" Dad asked.

"Beatrice hired her, and I must admit I had my reservations in the beginning, but Mary has more than proven herself. She pitches in wherever she can. My clients love her, and she takes great delight in showering my patients with attention."

"I don't know, son," his father said. "Don't get too involved with her. You need to be careful. The last thing you need is for her to learn of our family's shunning. The woman's liable to quit if she finds out."

Elijah felt a sinking feeling in his chest. What if his father was right? Would Mary leave work after she found out about his Amish past? And how would she learn the truth anyway?

It bothered him that he'd been unable to convince his family of Mary's worth. Only Jacob had met her and seen for himself how well she fit in the office. Jacob had told his family that Mary's cinnamon rolls had been fantastic, a melt-in-your-mouth treat. And Jacob had met her father and liked him. Mr. Troyer had treated Jacob with respect, which had gone a long way in his brother's mind in recognizing father and daughter's goodness and kindness as well as Mary's fine work ethic.

His father offered to slice the turkey. When his mother gave him a warm smile, Dad moved the bird from the countertop to his end of the table. The delicious aroma of turkey, stuffing, fresh bread and mashed potatoes filled the room, making him hungry. Mom handed Dad a carving knife, and as he began to slice the meat, the family conversation shifted to other things that didn't include Mary. He was glad Jacob hadn't mentioned Mary's mishap with her buggy.

Elijah sighed. He'd keep the image of her that night and afterward firmly in his thoughts where they belonged, but he was glad he'd be picking Mary up again on Monday morning. He tried to concentrate on their Thanksgiving dinner conversation, and for the most part, he succeeded. Until the time came for dessert, and his mother brought out Mary's cookies. And the Amish woman was again front and center in his mind.

When they were alone after dinner, Aaron grabbed his sleeve, his expression grave. "Don't fall for her, little brother. I heard what Jacob said. That you like her. You know it will work out horribly for you in the end if you expect her to be more than your employee."

"I'm not." Elijah experienced a tightening in his stomach, a pain that lasted until he got home and took two acetaminophen. While the tablets went to work, he watched TV. Anything to get through the weekend.

Don't get too involved with her. His father's words returned to haunt him and then Aaron's warning, *Don't fall for her, little brother.*

"Too late. I like her more than I should." Elijah didn't think Mary would quit her job after learning his family were shunned Amish. But he couldn't take the chance of telling her. Mary was the calming influence he needed whenever he was stressed, and he couldn't lose her.

A romantic relationship between them was a moot point since their lives were too different for them to be together as anything other than the employer/staff relationship they already had. Still, the memory of her sweet face and the warmth of her kind heart made him wish for more. The thought of having her in his life beyond work brought him a moment's happiness until it fluttered quickly away.

Chapter Twelve

Mary was standing outside in the cold waiting for him when Elijah pulled his car close to the house. He jumped out and hurried toward her after noticing the stack of foil containers in her arms.

"Aren't you freezing?" he asked with concern.

"I haven't been out here long," she assured him as he reached for the containers.

He smiled when she handed them to him. "I'm glad. I don't want you to get sick." They approached his car. "I can knock on your door, you know," he said. "I've done it before."

She chuckled. "I know."

Elijah was charmed by her good humor. But he worried about her, probably way more than he should. His family—mainly his parents and Aaron—had warned him not to get involved with Mary personally because she was Amish, and he'd assured them they were coworkers and friends, nothing more. But his sudden need to protect Mary from anything that could harm her or hurt her feelings had risen, changing him in ways he knew his father would tell him wasn't wise. Still, Mary was a good employee, and he wasn't about to lose her because of a temporary vet tech's inability to be nice to her.

"Did you have a nice weekend?"

Her lips twitched as she nodded. "I did, Dr. Zook. And you?"

"I spent Thanksgiving Day with my family and enjoyed myself." Mostly. Except for when his brother and parents tried to warn him to keep his distance from the Amish woman standing before him. "Didn't get enough turkey, though. I love it, don't you?"

She grinned. "I do."

He opened the car door on the passenger side for her. She got in and gazed up at him with a twinkle in her pretty blue eyes. "You're in a good mood this morning," he said, studying her as he handed her the food. "What did you bring?"

Mary chuckled. "Turkey with cranberry sauce and stuffing sandwiches and one container with dessert. But don't worry, everyone took home leftovers from a huge bird my mother cooked on Thanksgiving Day. This one was roasted yesterday. David's in-laws brought it over on Thursday when they came to dinner. Jonas told my mother that he knew there'd be no leftovers for our family because of the number of guests they had. He figured we could cook it whenever we wanted to enjoy another turkey meal. My mother decided to cook it on Saturday as we love turkey, and she didn't want to freeze it. The turkey and toppings on these sandwiches are from that second turkey meal my mother and I cooked."

"So, you're amused because I mentioned not having enough turkey," he murmured and saw her nod. After he carefully shut the car door, Elijah got into the vehicle on the other side. He pressed the ignition button, and the engine roared to life. As the car warmed up, he turned to study her beautiful features…the bright color of her eyes, her small nose that suited her and her nicely shaped, naturally pink lips. His family's warning faded far into the background.

He eyed the containers she held. "Why don't I put those containers on the back seat?"

She met his gaze with a smile. "They're fine where they are."

He nodded, then proceeded to turn his car around in the driveway before he pulled onto the road and headed toward the clinic. Elijah turned on the radio and flipped to a soft listening music station. As a song filled the car, he realized with a start that as an Amish woman, she probably wasn't allowed to listen to the radio. He recalled attending church with his family in his Old School Amish community where the only music they'd been allowed to sing were the songs from the *Ausbund* hymnal.

"Sorry," he murmured as he reached to turn off the radio.

"No, it's fine," she said, stopping him. "The music is lovely and soothing."

"If you're sure—"

"We're not allowed to own a radio, but there is no sin in listening to English music as long as we don't sing it around the house." She shifted in her seat. "It wouldn't bother my father to hear music in your office. Most medical facilities have it. We certainly don't ask them to turn it off."

Gazing ahead, he smiled. "Good to know."

The rest of the trip was made with a soft tune playing on the radio. Elijah didn't mind since her presence continued to soothe him. It wasn't until he parked the car and they entered the building that Mary spoke.

"I'll put these things in the break room," she said as she headed in that direction wearing her coat.

"What kind of dessert?" he asked, stopping her.

"Cookies, two slices of apple pie and a few lemon bars," she told him as she walked away.

Elijah smiled as he hung up his coat. The food she'd brought sounded delicious, and he was eager to taste everything.

The new vet assistant his brother loaned him came in through the back entrance.

"Morning, Dr. Zook," she greeted. "I'm Georgie. I'm filling in for Lacey until she returns on Wednesday. She's still visiting her family in New Jersey."

He nodded. "Thanks for assisting me today, Georgie. I appreciate your help," he told her. Then, together, they prepared the back room for the day.

Mary settled in at her desk after she'd turned on her laptop. She opened the schedule to make note of the number of patients who would be in today and when. At opening time, she unlocked the front door and returned to her seat.

The temporary vet tech entered her area. "I'm Georgie. Dr. Zook wants me to see who is coming in first and how many we have this morning," she said without inflection. Something in the young woman's brown eyes told her that Georgie didn't like her, and Mary had no idea what she could have done to offend her.

"I'll make a printout for you," Mary replied politely. She selected the time slot in the program and sent it to the printer. She rose and retrieved it, then handed it to Georgie with a smile. "There you go. If you need anything, let me know."

The tech accepted it without a smile or a thank you. Mary watched her leave, upset by the knowledge that she was working temporarily with someone who didn't try to be nice to her. She thought of Lacey, who'd been pleasant and fun...and who had quickly felt like a friend. Perhaps Georgie didn't want to be here. But why did the woman have to take it out on her? She wasn't the one who'd requested Georgie's help.

Mary forced Georgie's bad attitude from her mind and concentrated on her job. She smiled when the first patient and the owner entered. "Mrs. Wedermeier and Cooper! Good morning. I understand you're here for Cooper's first checkup." She stood and peered over the counter at the miniature long-haired dachshund. "What a cutie! I hear he's a gift from your husband."

"Yes." Mrs. Wedermeier beamed down at her pet. "John made a wonderful choice. I just love him. He's so adorable, even if he still has accidents in the house."

"He'll be fine once he's trained. Dr. Zook may be able to give you some tips." Mary checked Cooper in. "I'll let him know you're here."

But before Mary could call, Georgie came out of the back with a smile. "Mrs. Wedermeier! Dr. Zook is ready for you and Cooper. If you'll come with me…" The woman didn't look Mary's way as she brought Cooper and her owner into an exam room.

For the rest of the morning, the same thing happened. Georgie appeared and took owner and patient to an exam room without a word. Mary didn't know what the woman's problem was unless the tech just didn't like the Amish.

Soon, it was lunchtime. There was an hour between Elijah's last morning appointment and the first one of the afternoon. Closing out the current program she was working on, Mary went into the break room and brought out the turkey sandwiches she'd made, enough to feed three people. After placing each one on a paper plate, she put on a pot of coffee because she knew how much Elijah enjoyed it. The man himself came into the break room, made an exaggerated sniff of the coffee-scented air and then grinned at her as his gaze settled on the sandwiches.

"Everything looks and smells good in here," he commented, appearing pleased. Elijah pulled out a chair and sat down, studying the sandwich with curiosity.

"Have you never had stuffing and cranberry sauce on a turkey sandwich?" Mary asked with good humor.

"Can't say I have," he admitted before he picked up one half and took a bite. "Wow, that is good!"

She chuckled. "I'm glad you like it."

"Have a turkey sandwich," Elijah invited when Georgie entered the break room. "Mary made them, and they're delicious."

Georgie wrinkled her nose. "No, thanks. I've had enough turkey since Thanksgiving Day to last me a lifetime."

Mary frowned as she realized that the tech's comment was a dig at her. "Did you bring lunch?" she asked, managing to remain polite.

"No," the woman said without meeting Mary's gaze. "I wanted to let you know that I'm heading over to the store to pick up something." She addressed Elijah. "Do you want me to pick up anything for you while I'm out?"

Elijah shook his head as he took another bite, humming as he chewed. "I have everything I want or need right here. But thanks anyway."

Georgie left, and the room grew quiet. Mary poured Elijah coffee and set it within his reach.

Then she sat down and stared at her food, unable to understand why Georgie was continually rude to her.

"Mary?" Elijah's soft voice interrupted her thoughts.

She looked up and blinked until she saw his concerned expression. "Yes?"

"What's wrong?" he asked.

Mary shook her head, unwilling to speak ill of the assistant currently helping him. "I'm fine."

"Mary." His tone deepened as if he was determined to find out what was bothering her.

"I don't like to complain about anything, Elijah." She took a bite from her sandwich.

"Well, something isn't right," he said after a sip from his mug, "and I'd like to know what."

"Georgie," she murmured, blushing.

"What about her?" he asked, sounding curious.

"She's a good worker, isn't she?" Mary drank from her water bottle.

"She does the job." His intent study of her made her feel guilty.

"That's nice." Mary ate from her sandwich as the room grew quiet again, and the tension between them felt thick... at least, that was how she felt.

"Has she said something to you?" Elijah asked, breaking the silence.

Mary wouldn't meet his gaze. "When she first came in." She could sense his frown.

"She only spoke to you then?" He narrowed his eyes. "The woman works with you."

She shook her head. "Elijah, I'm not one to complain or tell tales."

He leaned closer to her side of the table. "Tell me."

Mary stared down at her sandwich, reluctant to tell him. "It's not something she said but the way she acts as if I'm not here."

"Look at me, Mary," he urged, and she lifted her head. "I want to know what's upset you."

"She ignores me. She dismisses me and my role in the office." She felt her face heat. "It's fine. She's a good worker, and you need her. I'll continue to be nice to her in the hopes that she'll acknowledge me with a smile." Mary got up and grabbed a container filled with desserts. "Try a lemon bar or a cookie," she invited. "Or if you'd prefer, you can try a slice of apple pie and save the other treats for later."

"I'll have a lemon bar," he said, and she saw him smile when she put one on a small paper plate and handed it to him.

Mary's good humor returned with the absence of Georgie, but she knew the tech would be back soon with her lunch. She decided to enjoy the peaceful interlude before the woman's return. *At least Georgie isn't a permanent hire.* If she was, Mary didn't know how she'd cope with the tech's poor attitude and rudeness toward her long-term.

Georgie didn't come back until after she and Elijah finished their lunch and were ready to head back to work.

The afternoon went much like the morning had. Georgie came out for a patient before Mary had a chance to let her know that the pet and owner were here. But later that afternoon, close to an hour from closing time, a repeat client came in with a new patient, a blue cockatiel.

"Hello, Judy," Mary greeted. "Did you get yourself a new bird?"

Judy grinned. "I most certainly did. It belonged to my son who's off to college and couldn't take Margie." She held up the small traveling cage. "I want to make sure she's healthy and find out what I should do to keep her that way. Jimmy hasn't had her long, so I'd like to know what's best for her."

"Dr. Zook can help you with that." Mary wondered why Georgie hadn't shown up yet. She'd come out front on her own all day. "If you'll have a seat, I'll let him know that you're here."

The older woman nodded, then sat down.

Still, there was no Georgie. Mary rose from her chair and went to the back to tell Elijah his next patient was here. She found him in his office. "Judy is here with Margie, her son's cockatiel. She's watching the bird while he's away in school, and she wants to make sure she knows how to properly care for her."

Elijah smiled. "Thanks, Mary. Bring her to exam room one, please."

She returned his smile and did what he asked her. Georgie entered the exam room after Mary had settled Judy and Margie inside. "I would have come out front if you'd wanted," the tech hissed under her breath as Mary walked by.

She went back to her desk, fighting tears. Georgie's unpleasant behavior had gotten to her. Mary was glad she'd be leaving with Elijah at the end of the day.

Georgie was all smiles as she escorted Judy and the bird to the front door. The tech knew that Mary needed to check out all patients; yet, Georgie had bypassed the front desk with their last patient as if Mary's job meant nothing. Mary wasn't worried about Judy's payment. She knew the woman would settle up.

Georgie glared at her as she walked by on the way to the back room. Mary decided she needed a cookie to feel better after the bad day she'd endured.

"Have a good night, Dr. Zook," Mary heard the tech say to Elijah when Mary was in the break room. "I'll see you tomorrow."

Mary sighed and reached for a second treat to help ease the anxiety after a trying day dealing with Georgie.

Elijah entered the break room. "Have you got any more of those cookies?" he asked, nodding at the closed container.

She slid the cookie container in his direction after he'd sat down. "There's also apple pie, remember."

"Cookies first. The pie will keep until tomorrow, right?" He took a bite of a chocolate chip cookie. "I love these."

Mary tried to smile. "I'm glad. I can make more over the winter."

"I should bring us something delicious to munch on." He was quiet as he chewed and swallowed. She could feel him watching her as she poured him a coffee and still while he reached for another cookie.

"Tell me what's wrong," he urged. "And don't tell me it's nothing."

"Georgie will be here to help out tomorrow," she said, but there must have been something in her tone that suggested she was unhappy about it.

"I watched her," he confessed, surprising her. "She was pleasant enough to work with in the back with me, but I didn't like the way she acted toward you."

"Elijah—"

"No, Mary. I heard her when you brought Judy and her bird into the room. She sounded angry that you were doing your job."

She felt the intensity of his gaze. "Georgie doesn't like me," she whispered. "And I don't know why."

"I didn't see it at first, but it's not like you to be quiet and closed off." Elijah's expression was apologetic. "We don't have to put up with that. *You* don't have to put up with her."

Mary blinked back tears that he cared enough to be concerned. "But you need her help. You said yourself she is a skilled, capable vet tech."

"She may know her job, but that doesn't make her a good employee." Elijah placed a hand over hers on the table before he quickly withdrew it as if he'd done something wrong. "I'll call Jacob. Lacey was supposed to start on Wednesday. I'll see if she can work tomorrow and the rest of the week."

"Thank you." She looked up at him with gratitude. "I like Lacey."

"I do, too, but mostly because I saw how friendly the two of you were. Everyone who works here must be kind and a good fit. Hopefully, we'll find a permanent hire who's like Lacey." He drank the last swallow of coffee. "Are you ready to go home?"

"I will be as soon as I shut down my computer," she said, feeling so much better now because of Elijah's understanding of her bad day.

Soon, she and Elijah were in his car, heading toward her house. "I... You know my *dat* is going to ask when you can make it for a meal."

He didn't look away from the road, yet she saw a flicker in the dashboard light that suggested doubt in his eyes.

Mary slumped in her seat, disappointed. She'd wanted him to have a meal with her family, although having him at their dinner table might seem like they were crossing the line between employer and employee.

"Let me check my calendar, and I'll let you know when I can come," he said, facing her for a brief second.

Her spirits rose at his response. "Okay."

She was eager to see Elijah interact more with her family. And she refused to look too closely for the reason why that would make her so happy. Because it would hint at something that wasn't possible although she wished differently.

Chapter Thirteen

Elijah grew thoughtful as he drove to Mary's the next morning. While Georgie had been perfectly pleasant with him yesterday, he'd sensed something cold underlying the tech's tone toward Mary that bothered him. Mary had been quiet and unwilling to tell him what had upset her. It was clear that she'd had a bad day, which was odd because she seemed always to be happy lately, especially since they'd started to work more closely. He'd phoned Jacob last night to request Lacey's help if she was back from out of state. It was important that his staff worked well together.

As he parked near her house, the side door opened and Mary exited the residence. She appeared somber until he got out of the car to open the door for her. Then, her lips tilted slightly in a smile. "Good morning, Elijah."

"Good morning," he told her as he helped her inside. He noticed that today she wasn't carrying any food items, no breakfast or baked goods, as if she was feeling off.

"I'm sorry," she said, "I didn't bake anything for today."

"You don't have to always bring food, Mary," he assured her with a smile, wondering how she'd known what he was thinking. "And there are still snacks in the refrigerator."

Mary appeared relieved. He shut her door after she'd settled inside and went around to the driver's side.

Once in the car, he faced her with concern. "Are you all right? Do you need a day off?"

She blinked. "No, I'm fine."

"If you're sure…"

She nodded.

The heat was on in the clinic as Elijah hung up his coat and offered to take hers. Mary gave him her woolen coat willingly before she left the area. He went to his office and turned on the light. Hearing noise in the break room, he found Mary making coffee. He was silent as he watched her. She had already searched the refrigerator and set the desserts she'd brought yesterday onto the table. When she was done, she seemed startled when she turned and saw him. "I'm sorry. I didn't realize you were standing there."

"I hope I didn't startle you," he said softly.

She shrugged. "I thought at first that you were Georgie."

He nodded, understanding. "No Georgie. Just me."

Mary gave him a small smile. "I'll be out front if you need me."

The day for Mary got a whole lot better once she realized that it was Lacey and not Georgie helping out at the office today. She'd been stunned when Lacey walked into the clinic, back from vacation and ready to work. The women exchanged pleasantries and Mary's mood brightened considerably. She made new entries into the electronic medical charts. It wasn't until she sensed him standing there that she looked up. "Elijah."

He smiled. "So, Lacey is here with us the rest of the week."

She nodded vigorously in response. "It's good to have her back."

"I feel the same." He studied her silently for a long moment, but she didn't feel uncomfortable for some reason. "I called Jacob last night and asked him to replace Georgie with Lacey." His expression softened, and he stood. "She was back from her trip and available." He flashed her a smile. "Was that okay?"

Mary smiled and couldn't stop. "It's more than okay." He nodded, and then, his lips curving, he turned to leave. Then he faced her once more.

"Yesterday you were a professional despite the difficulties. I need you, Mary." He continued quickly as if the last part had made him uncomfortable. "You're a valued employee. That fact alone is something to celebrate."

Mary's heart thumped at his words, and with the warmth in his eyes she felt as if the two of them had crossed the line. Something seemed to be happening between them that shouldn't. "Thank you, Elijah," she replied.

Lunch turned out to be calzones. Mary had never tasted a calzone before. It was made from pizza dough and stuffed with different things like ham and ricotta cheese, sausage and peppers, or whatever you wanted to have inside. She ate one with the ham and cheese.

After lunch, Mary was back at her desk, prepared to work through the rest of the afternoon on bookkeeping and ordering the list of supplies Elijah had given her earlier. It was nice to know that he trusted her enough to do that for him, although it was easy enough for her to do since she had the companies he used with their phone numbers.

Mary looked up when she heard the front door open. Simeon walked in with Snowflake snuggled in his blanket in the cardboard box Elijah had given her father last week.

"Simeon." She greeted him with a smile, then went into the waiting room to love on his puppy. "How's he doing?" she asked. "Has he eaten anything today?"

"A little chicken and rice, but not much," her brother said.

"I'm hoping Dr. Zook will suggest something else to get Snowflake to eat more."

Lacey entered the front desk area. "Mary?"

Mary waved at her friend. "I'm out here! Come and meet my brother's puppy."

Lacey approached with a smile as soon as she saw the small dog in the box Simeon was holding. "Adorable!" she exclaimed. "I didn't know you owned a puppy."

"Snowflake isn't mine. He belongs to Simeon, my younger brother. Lacey, this is Simeon. Sim, this is Lacey, my friend, and the vet tech working with us today."

"Are you ready for me to take you into an exam room?" Lacey asked him with a smile. "Follow me."

They disappeared into the back room, but it wasn't long before Lacey brought Simeon and Snowflake back out to the reception desk.

"Dr. Zook said there's no charge today for Snowflake's care," Lacey told her.

"I should pay," Simeon insisted.

"He won't let you, *bruder*," Mary said with a grin. "It's because you're my brother, and I work here. Don't worry, he has a sweet tooth and happens to like my baked goods. I'll make sure he gets enough to keep him happy and satisfy his hunger."

Simeon nodded. "*Okey.*"

"I'll carry the dog food and walk you out," Lacey said, holding two cans of wet puppy food. She turned to Mary. "Dr. Zook wants to see Snowflake again on Friday or even sooner if your brother can't get him to eat this."

"Dr. Zook thinks that this new food will tempt Snowflake into eating," Simeon said as he gazed at the puppy in his arms.

Carrying the sample cans of food, Lacey followed Simeon out through the front entrance. She was back within seconds with a smile. "I hope Snowflake is all right," she said. "He's so tiny. The good thing is that he doesn't seem to be sick. Dr. Zook thinks the antibiotics he gave him last week helped to revive him."

Mary nodded, grateful that the puppy might be turning a corner.

The rest of the afternoon flew by with back-to-back appointments, and soon it was time to leave. Elijah entered her area a few minutes after Lacey left for the night. "Are you ready to go?"

She nodded.

"All set," she said after grabbing her cape from the closet and put it around her shoulders. Dressed in warm clothes, she followed him out to his car. He was quiet, but she figured it was because he was tired. They'd enjoyed only one short break at lunch to eat their calzones.

Elijah unlocked and opened the car door for her. He waited until she was fully inside before he closed it. He still wasn't talking as he usually did, and she wondered if something else was bothering him. Mary wanted to ask, but she knew it was none of her business.

Once in the driver's seat, he started the car and pulled out of the parking lot onto the road toward her house.

"Thanks for lunch today," she said cheerfully. "I'd never had a calzone before. It tasted wonderful. I was so full, I left half of it for tomorrow." When he didn't respond, she worried that she'd been talking too much.

Elijah finally glanced at her briefly. "I liked mine, too. I'm a good eater, but I couldn't finish mine either."

"Lacey worked out today," she said.

He smiled. "She is a hard worker, and she's pleasant." Elijah kept his eyes on the road for a moment. "So, your brother reminded me that I've accepted an invitation to your house for dinner."

"Oh… I'm sorry if he pestered you about it," she said with concern. "But I have no doubt it was my father who urged Simeon to push for a date for you to come."

"No need to apologize," he replied, still without looking at her. "Simeon had different dates in mind. I checked my schedule and told him I could be there on Wednesday, a week from tomorrow."

"Are you sure?" she questioned, worried about forcing him to join a family meal. He still seemed hesitant about it, and she wondered why.

His attention back on the road, he said, "Just let me know what time I need to be there."

"Okay." Mary saw that they had arrived at her home already. Elijah pulled into the driveway and turned his car around to face the road. "Thanks for the ride."

She opened the door to get out.

"Mary," he called, drawing her attention. "I won't be able to pick you up tomorrow, as I have an appointment first thing. Will you be able to get a ride in?"

Hiding her disappointment about the morning, she nodded. "I'll ask Dat to drive me." She still wasn't ready to drive herself.

"I can still drive you home after work," he assured her.

As Mary walked toward the house, Elijah drove away without waiting for her to enter as he usually did. And he'd been way too quiet as he took her home.

Worried why his behavior toward her had changed, she still managed a smile as she greeted her mother. "*Hallo*, Mam! I'm home."

She continued to be concerned throughout the evening with her family and as she got ready for bed. Then it occurred to her he might have something important to do. And Elijah did promise to drive her home after work tomorrow. But despite how his concern about Georgie's behavior touched her, Mary became determined to keep her distance and be professional so she didn't get her hopes up about the possibility of meaning more to him.

Chapter Fourteen

As he pulled his car into the lot next to the New Berne Animal Hospital, Elijah noticed there were no other vehicles parked there. And there were no lights on inside the building that he could see. Still, he knew his brother would be here since Jacob had called him yesterday at the clinic to ask if he could stop by this morning. Jacob had something he wanted to discuss with him.

He went to the door his brother had told him would be unlocked. He entered the hospital, calling Jacob's name.

Jacob came out from a room. "Great, you're here. Come on back." He turned, and Elijah followed him.

"Nice office, brother," he said, taking the seat on the opposite side of Jacob's large wooden desk. "Did you buy new furniture?" He'd only been in his brother's domain one time; Jacob and he were usually too busy seeing patients to visit each other at work.

Jacob shrugged. "It's a new desk. Does the job and all but I'd be happy with less."

Elijah smiled. It was so like this brother not to be impressed by money or material things. The only thing that mattered to Jacob was caring for animals, especially horses. He leaned back in his chair. "So, what did you want to talk with me about?"

His brother smiled. "How is Lacey making out?"

"She's great. A real pro, and she gets along with everyone," Elijah said. "Thanks so much for loaning her to me."

"What would you say if you could hire her permanently?" Jacob watched Elijah closely as he waited for him to answer.

"What? Are you serious?" Elijah was stunned. "Is that possible?"

His brother nodded. "Lacey came to see me after leaving your clinic yesterday. She'd already told me she lives close to your practice. After helping at your clinic, she confessed that she prefers working at your place with the pets rather than livestock." Jacob stretched with his arms raised over his head. "So, what do you think? The fact that you're impressed with her tells me that you like the idea of hiring her."

"I do, but what about you?" Elijah asked. "How will her leaving affect your staff?" Having Lacey on board permanently took a load off his mind.

"We'll be fine." Jacob rose. "Want any coffee? I'm longing for a cup."

"That would be great." Elijah needed the caffeine. Usually he was fine until he got to the office, but he was going to be late.

Jacob left the room and returned with a steaming cup of brew in each hand. He set one on his desk in front of Elijah with the fixings his brother knew Elijah preferred. Seated again, Jacob made a sound of appreciation after he took his first sip of coffee. "I needed that."

Elijah regarded him with a small smile. "Me, too." The scent teased his nostrils as he drank from his cup before setting it down. "So, tell me more about Lacey and her desire to work for me."

"She likes working in a much smaller facility, and your place is only a couple of miles from her house." Jacob opened his desk drawer, pulled out two wrapped bars and tossed one to Elijah. "Chocolate chunk granola bar. Gives you energy with a sweet taste." He opened his own and took a bite, chewing it and swallowing before he went on. "So... Lacey... If you offer to hire her, I guarantee she'll accept." He drank from his coffee.

Elijah nodded. "She is a good worker," he admitted thoughtfully. "And she and Mary have become instant friends." He shifted again, uncomfortable. "It's important my staff work well together."

Jacob eyed him solemnly at the mention of his receptionist. "There is something else I'd like to discuss. Or should I say some*one*."

Elijah frowned as concern caused a tightening in his chest. "Mary?"

Jacob nodded. "Mary."

"What about her?" He didn't want to discuss the woman for whom he'd unwillingly started to care for. It wasn't as if he could ever act on it.

"You like her," Jacob said as he had once before. "As in you like-like her."

"She's my employee," Elijah replied, hoping to sound convincing.

"So? She's also a lovely young woman who is a good worker." His brother studied him silently for a long moment. "Who bakes for you and accepts a ride from you every day."

"And what's wrong with that? She brings in food for everyone." This conversation about Mary was making his heart race. "And since her accident, I feel better driving her." He didn't want to talk about her...with anyone.

"Eli, I know what Mom, Dad and Aaron said to you, warning you not to get involved with her." Jacob studied him with compassionate blue eyes.

"They're right," Elijah replied quickly. "She is Amish. I'm

not. We've had to live the English life, not because we chose it, but because we were shunned and thrown out of our community." He'd found it hard to have a meaningful relationship since being rejected that way as a child.

"You know, I've been thinking a lot about that time in our lives, and I can't seem to accept that what our elders did to us was the right thing to do." Jacob drank from his cup. "We were children, Eli. Innocent children. There was no bad intent in what Aaron did in picking up the cell phone. The only thing he wanted to do was return it to its owner!"

Elijah experienced an overwhelming moment of sadness. "I know. I tried to talk with the church elders after it happened, but they refused to listen. As far as they were concerned, we'd been shunned and thus should be ignored like we'd never existed."

"I didn't know you went to see them," Jacob said with regret.

"No one knew. I felt hurt and ashamed." Elijah remembered how bad he'd felt when the church elders he'd wanted to talk with had acted like he hadn't existed. As a child, it was his first inkling how bad it was going to be if his family had continued to live in their farmhouse.

Jacob shook his head. "I'm sorry you went through that." He leaned back in his chair. "I wonder if the same elders are still in charge. Not that it matters."

"I cared about that for a long time but no longer. That part of our lives is still too painful to remember." Elijah exhaled sharply. "They were supposed to be men of God. I'm not sure there was anything blessed or godly about any one of them."

Jacob nodded. "Which brings me back to Mary. She lives in a different Amish community than ours. She's friendly and warm while the women in Big Valley were stoic and strict in order to keep their children in line. I've met Mary's father. He's a pleasant fellow. I imagine the whole family is warmhearted."

"They are," he admitted reluctantly. "I've met her parents and brothers. I'm supposed to have dinner at their house next week."

"There you have it!" Jacob exclaimed. "If Mary knew what happened to our family and she accepted it, would you be willing to pursue a relationship with her?"

"She's Amish, Jake!" The thought of telling her the truth about their shunning made it difficult for him to breathe. "She wouldn't understand." And if their parents knew, they'd encourage her to distance herself from him.

"And we were Amish once," his brother said. "I've seen the way Mary looks at you. I may be wrong but I don't think your feelings are one-sided. There's a good chance Mary likes you as much as you do her. Trust her to accept whatever you tell her about our past without judgment."

"And if she doesn't?" Elijah asked. "What if she learns the truth and decides that she can no longer work for a shunned Amish man?"

"You weren't a man when you were shunned, Eli," Jacob reminded him. "You were a ten-year-old boy." He glanced toward the wall clock. "Say something to her or not, it's up to you. But it's getting late, and you need to get to work." He narrowed his gaze. "But know this, we are not done with our discussion about you and Mary."

Ignoring his brother's last statement, Elijah stood. "Thanks for telling me about Lacey. I'll talk with her as soon as I see her." He finished his coffee. "Where do you want this?" he asked as he held up his mug.

Jacob rose as well. "Leave it. I'll see that it's washed and put away."

"Thanks, Jacob," Elijah said.

"For the coffee *and the advice*, right?" his brother prompted with a laugh.

"No comment. Now I know Mary is the reason you really wanted to see me today." His brother's words had given him hope where he was sure there should be none.

"See you at our folks a week from Sunday?" Jacob murmured as he accompanied Elijah to the door.

Elijah nodded, acknowledging the planned dinner with their family. "I'll be there."

As he drove away from Jacob's office, his discussion with Jacob about Mary made him apprehensive, a feeling he continued to fight as he headed to the clinic. Why should he risk telling her about the shunning? What if she learned the truth and left because she couldn't accept it?

His anxiety spiked when he saw the light on in the front area of the building. Mary was already at her desk, working hard. *I can't tell her.* He would lose her if he did.

"Hi, Mary!" Lacey entered the reception area with a smile. Mary looked up from her computer. "Good morning!"

"Any idea where Dr. Zook is?" the tech asked.

"He told me he had an early appointment, but he didn't say where it was." Mary stretched in her chair. "I'm sure he'll be here at any moment."

The young woman grinned. "I hope so. We won't be able to see patients without him." She pulled out Beatrice's chair and sat down. "Did you hear that we're expecting snow today?"

Mary frowned. "I didn't. How much?"

Before the tech could answer, they heard movement in the back room. "Dr. Zook?" Lacey called out.

Elijah appeared in the doorway. "It's me," he said. "Good morning." He barely looked at Mary before his gaze settled on his temporary assistant. "Lacey, would you come into my office?"

Lacey exchanged worried glances with Mary. "Sure. I'll be right there."

Mary saw him nod before he left the room. "What do you think that's about, Lacey?"

And why he hadn't looked her in the eye...

Lacey shrugged, but Mary could tell that she was nervous. "I have no idea... Unless...he doesn't need me here anymore."

"I don't think that's it," Mary said to ease Lacey's fear. "Why would he let you go?"

The vet tech sighed heavily. "I better get back there before we start receiving patients." Lacey headed toward Elijah's office, and Mary feared that she'd lose her coworker and new friend.

Mary concentrated on her work, yet her thoughts returned to Lacey in Elijah's office.

Moments later, Lacey came out with a huge smile on her face. "Guess what? Dr. Zook just hired me permanently!" she exclaimed with happiness shining in her brown eyes.

"That's wonderful!" Mary gasped, pleased. With Lacey working here full-time, things would go smoothly, and they'd get more done. "How did this come about?"

"I mentioned I was interested in working here to Dr. Zook's brother, and he told Dr. Zook!" Lacey couldn't stop grinning. "Oh, and our boss wants to see you in his office next."

Mary's heart thundered in her chest, and her hands felt damp as she became more nervous. She reached his office and paused at the open doorway. "Elijah? You wanted to see me?"

He looked up. "Come in, Mary."

She nodded and entered.

"Please shut the door," he said.

She obeyed and sat down in the chair he indicated across from him. "Is something wrong?"

He widened his eyes. "No, no! I'm sorry you were worried. I just wanted to tell you about hiring Lacey and about Betty, who will be in tomorrow to fill out paperwork for her employment. Both have agreed to work full-time."

Mary grinned. "Wonderful! I'm happy for both of them."

"They will make it less stressful for us," he told her. "You can open the door now." He rose. "I bought doughnuts today. I know they won't be as good as yours, but I figured they'd still be a good treat for the office." He waved her ahead of him. "Is there coffee? If not, I'll make some."

"I made some a little while ago," she said as she preceded him to the break room.

"Thanks." He poured himself a cup and then helped himself to a cream-filled doughnut with chocolate on the top. "Tell Lacey to come and join us. We have time, don't we?"

"We have a half hour before our day begins in earnest." Mary hurried to find Lacey, who still stood in the reception area. "Lacey, Dr. Zook brought doughnuts. He said to come back and have some with coffee. But if you'd prefer tea, I can make you that as well."

"Coffee and doughnuts." Lacey's eyes glowed. "Sounds perfect to me." She glanced out the window. "It's already snowing hard."

The trio settled in for a coffee break, which was quickly followed by their first appointment cancellation, followed by another. With the weather worsening over the course of the morning, Elijah eventually decided to close up early. He let Lacey go and offered to drive Mary home. She stood near the front desk later that morning, watching the snow falling fast as drifts started to form in the parking lot. "Mary," Elijah said, approaching her from behind. "Are you all right?"

She nodded. "I didn't realize how much snow we've gotten."

His expression seemed to soften as he studied her. "Give me a moment, and we can close shop. At least it's still daylight, which should help with visibility as I take you home."

"I'll shut down the computer and lock the front door," Mary told him and then hurried to do just that.

When she was done, she returned to the back area. Elijah joined her seconds later.

He took her coat off the hanger and handed it to her. "Bundle up. The wind is picking up."

As he dressed in warm outer clothing, Mary pulled her scarf, gloves and bonnet from inside her coat sleeves and donned them after she put on her coat and fastened the clasps to keep it closed.

"Ready?" Elijah asked.

She nodded.

"Good," he said. "Wait here while I bring the car closer to the door."

Before Mary could tell him that she could follow him, he ran out into the cold and got into his vehicle. He pulled up close to the building and opened the passenger door for her when she stepped outside. She immediately felt the force of the wind sending snow into her face. Face red, he waited patiently for her to get inside before he closed the door and ran around the rear of the car to get into the driver's seat. The windshield wipers made a swish-swish sound as the blades moved back and forth rhythmically, helping to clear snow from the glass so Elijah could see better. For a moment, her thoughts went to her accident with snowfall as heavy as this one.

But the best thing Mary noticed was the wonderful heat

that blasted from the vents on the front dashboard, taking away the chill.

"Warm enough?" he asked softly.

"Yes," she murmured as she hugged herself with her arms.

"You're remembering your accident," he said with a tenderness that drew her attention. "I'll keep you safe. Don't worry. We'll take it slow. The roads have only an inch or two. It's the wind that makes it seem worse. I'll get you home safely." His concern for her was evident in his caring expression as he met her gaze. "Trust me?"

She felt captured by his blue gaze. "Yes," she said without hesitation.

"Good." He sounded pleased.

As promised, Elijah drove carefully, his eyes on the road. Mary could tell he checked, from time to time, for a sign of any vehicles or buggies that might be parked on the side of the road or traveling along the shoulder.

Mary felt safe in his car. But she couldn't help but be concerned about him heading home through bad weather after he dropped her off. And her fear for his safety as the snow was tossed about in the wind was more terrifying to her than anything she'd felt in a long while.

He turned into her driveway and pulled up close to her house. When he started to get out of the car, she stopped him. "No need for you to get wetter than you already are," she said.

"Mary—"

"I'll be fine," she assured him, placing her hand on the door handle. "But I don't like you having to go home in all this. Do you want to come inside to warm up before you go?"

"I'd better not," he said. "Better to get home now before the storm worsens."

She didn't like it, but she understood his reasoning. "Will you let me know once you get home?"

Elijah didn't say anything at first. It seemed like more than minutes passed before he finally nodded. He looked toward the house and noticed that the door was open with Mary's mother waiting for her. "You best get inside before your mother catches a cold."

Mary glanced over and saw her *mam* behind the screened door. "Thank you for the ride, Elijah," she whispered, meeting his gaze.

"You're welcome, Mary," he said before he gestured toward her door. "I can still open that door for you."

"No need." Mary swung open the door and immediately experienced the bite of the wind and the sting of the blowing snow. She ran toward the house and in through the open front door.

When she glanced back to the car, Elijah was already driving away.

"It looks bad out there," her *mam* said.

"It is," she agreed. "He wanted to get out and open the door for me, but I told him to stay in the car. No sense him getting cold and soaked to the skin before he drives home."

Her mother eyed her with a funny look.

"What?" Mary asked.

"You're worried about him," she said.

"*Ja*, of course, I am. The weather is terrible, and he must drive home in it."

"*Dat* went over to get your *grosseldre*. Although they are not going to like it, I'll not have my parents staying in their cottage alone. They need to be here with us."

Mary agreed as she undid the clasps on her woolen coat.

Mam didn't say another thing as she helped Mary pull off her coat and tuck her bonnet and gloves into a sleeve. "Tea?"

"*Ja*, please, Mam." As she thought of Elijah, she felt her face heat. She could only hope that her mother would attribute the redness to the cold wind. Mary rubbed her hands together to warm them as her mother turned the burner under the kettle, and she sent up a silent prayer that the man she cared about—her English boss—would arrive safely home and then call her as promised.

Chapter Fifteen

Mary and her family ate a simple supper of chicken soup with crackers. As she helped her mother wash and dry dishes, she kept her phone close, hoping Elijah would call soon. But after two hours passed without hearing from him, she grew increasingly upset, fearing that something bad had happened.

"What's wrong, *dochter*?" her mother asked when Mary closed her eyes to send up a silent prayer for Elijah's safety.

"I haven't heard from Dr. Zook," Mary replied with worry, "and he said he'd call to let me know when he got home safely." Fear made her panic. She needed to know if he was all right.

"Call him then," Mam said. "Maybe it took longer than he thought to get home. And it's possible he just got in."

"*Okey*. I'll call him," she replied. Still, she was hesitant to call a man and an Englisher at that; but her concern for him had her dialing his number. Her mother left the kitchen, giving her privacy to talk with him. She waited what seemed like a long time for Elijah to answer until he finally picked up after several rings.

"Hello?" he said in greeting.

"Elijah! You're all right!" She breathed a sigh of relief. Not hearing from him had made her fear that he'd had an accident like she had but with a more serious outcome.

"Mary, I'm so sorry that I didn't call you." He sounded

sincere and suddenly more alert. "It took forever for me to drive home with snow blowing everywhere. When I got here, I needed to warm up, so I made coffee and started my supper. I wanted to call you before I ate, but I was afraid that you were in the middle of dinner."

"As long as you're all right," she whispered, close to tears of relief.

"Mary," he murmured. "I didn't mean to worry you."

She sniffed without saying anything.

"I'm sorry," he said, sounding sincere. "I honestly meant to call."

"I know," she said. "And I'm fine. But after my accident, all I could think about was you might have had one. And that you were lying in a ditch somewhere unconscious."

"Mary... I'm sorry," he repeated. "I'm well, and my car doesn't have a scratch." There was silence on his end for a moment.

"I'm glad you are home safe and sound, Elijah," she told him, brightening as it finally sunk in that he was okay. Mary sent a prayer of thanks up to *Gott*, grateful her fears had been unfounded. "I...was truly worried about you." The silence that settled between them was thick with tension and strong feelings. She needed to break it before she said something she shouldn't. "Will you let me know if anything changes with office hours and the weather tomorrow?"

"I will." His voice was so soft that she almost couldn't hear it. "I already called the radio station about the closing. I'll change the clinic's answering machine message and dial in remotely to check for calls/"

"Thank you." She briefly closed her eyes as she leaned back against the kitchen counter. "I should let you go..."

"Mary? May I call you tomorrow?" He paused. "I can give you an update."

She nodded, thrilled that he would call her again soon. "Yes, that would be good. Thank you."

"What did you have for supper?" Elijah asked in a sudden switch of topic.

Mary found herself smiling. Neither one of them was ready to end the call.

"Chicken corn chowder and we had ham and cheese sandwiches," she told him as she heard him moving around on the other end of the line. He'd eaten supper, so was he looking for dessert? "Elijah? Where did you learn to speak Amish?" Mary waited to hear his answer but he was silent a long moment before replying.

"I've lived here in New Berne for some time," he finally said.

"I thought it might be that. Still, I was surprised when I realized you knew some words."

His chuckle over the line gave her pleasure. "Not everyone speaks English in an Englisher's company."

"I'm sure you're right." Although she didn't want to hang up, she realized that staying on the line suggested something between them that wasn't there. "I should let you go, Elijah." Her voice softened to a whisper. "And have a good night's sleep."

"The same to you, Mary," he said, and she sensed him smile. "I'll call you tomorrow."

"Sounds good. Have a nice night," she told him.

There was a silent pause as if he, like she, wasn't ready to hang up, and then she heard a definite click as he ended the call.

Elijah took a bite of the cupcake he'd found for dessert, following it with a swallow of milk. As he sat in the living room, gazing at the television, his thoughts centered only on

Mary. He like-liked her, just as Jacob had suggested. He was falling for her, a mistake since their lives were so different from each other. Still, he had been Amish once. But what if she was willing to give him a chance? Even after he told her about the shunning?

Tell her, Jacob had said. And then what? Have her look at him like the shunned little boy who was now an adult and turn away?

Lately, thoughts of her possible rejection hurt. He'd dated in the past, but he hadn't been invested in a relationship with the women he'd seen casually. His heart had been too closed for anyone else before her. His feelings for Mary were stronger but with the differences in their lifestyles, there was little chance that they could have a future.

Once he finished with his dessert, Elijah threw out his cupcake paper and washed his empty glass, remembering the exact moment she'd called him, her voice anxious. She'd been worried. The terrible feeling he'd had when she'd first spoken had settled like a rock in his stomach. He'd honestly meant to call her first thing. Then, like a fool, he'd delayed, hurting Mary by not keeping his promise.

Elijah flipped on the outside light and peered out the door window. He frowned. The storm had taken a turn for the worse. It was December, when they often had heavy snowfalls, but the severity of this storm was different. The original forecast had called for snow but nothing like this, with the wind blustering, creating blizzard-like conditions. Odds were every business in the area would be shut down tomorrow and probably the day after that. He wondered what Jacob thought and picked up the phone to call his brother.

"Hey, it's me," he said when his brother answered. "Looks like our winter storm's become a blizzard, doesn't it?"

"Yeah, the snow's coming down hard, and the wind is

blowing it everywhere," Jacob said. "I can barely see a thing outside my apartment."

"Is the hospital closed tomorrow?" He leaned back in his chair and stared at the ceiling.

"No doubt," Jacob predicted. "Yours?"

"Unless there is a big improvement, which I doubt will happen, we'll be closed and stay that way until further notice. No one wants to venture out in these conditions anyway. Let's hope everything stays quiet," Elijah continued. "What happens if there is an emergency?"

"I'll either handle it myself or one of my partners will," his brother said, making Elijah feel better about not being able to drive in to open the clinic. Jacob's SUV could handle the snow but the wind could still make it difficult.

"I'll make sure all calls are forwarded to my cell phone to see if it's something simple like clients' questions about their pets." He hated to hang up. Elijah hoped that there were no emergencies. "I'll let you go, Jake. Get some sleep, brother. Check in tomorrow?"

"I'll call you." Jacob grew quiet for a moment. "Have you told Mary about our past yet?"

"No," Elijah said. "I'm not ready to tell her. I don't want to lose her."

"I think you're making a mistake, Elijah. You can have her in your life if only you'd take a chance."

"I can't, Jacob," he said sadly. "I just can't." But he desperately wanted to believe she'd understand.

"Suit yourself, brother," Jacob replied, clearly upset with his decision. "But don't think this conversation between you and me is over. I can see that Mary is too important to you for me to let it go."

After they ended the call, Elijah sat at the table, going over what his brother had said. Maybe he should listen to Jacob and tell her everything soon. He'd never have her in any way if he kept it a secret. But with his past, he'd never be allowed to join the Amish faith. Was it possible that Mary, a kind and compassionate woman, would listen to the truth and understand? And if she cared for him as much as he loved her, would she even consider living an English life with him?

Elijah returned to his living room sofa and searched the guide until he found a documentary on the life of African jungle animals—anything to escape his thoughts after talking with Jacob. He woke up still on the sofa to utter darkness and realized the power was out and must have been out for some time because it was chilly in the house. His heat pump was out. Thankfully, he had a fireplace that could provide enough heat to keep him warm if he stayed in the room. He'd been taught to make a fire when he was a boy. It was one of the many skills he'd learned while living the Amish way of life that came in handy. He kept dry logs on the grate for whenever he was in the mood to enjoy his fireplace. He grabbed a newspaper from a rack, crumpled it and tucked it in with the wood. Using a long match, he lit the paper and watched as the fire spread to engulf the logs with an instant feeling of warmth. He grabbed a pillow and his quilt from the sofa and then lay on the floor near the fireplace.

He closed his eyes, hoping to fall back to sleep, but the wind whipping against the siding of his house was fierce. He wondered how Mary and her family were making out in the cold. Were they still in their beds or huddled close to their great room wood-burning stove?

He stared into the fire, his thoughts on Mary, as he began to wonder if Jacob was right. Maybe he should tell her about his Amish past. It would be a gift if she listened and understood.

Elijah tried to stay awake, but exhaustion took hold of him, and he drifted back to sleep. And he dreamt of Mary. He woke up abruptly, feeling disoriented as he was jolted from the dream, and experienced an intense longing to see the Amish woman with the bright blue eyes and sweet, genuine smile.

The power was restored when he got up the next day. He checked his voicemail and learned that several calls had come through. He called each client back, assuring them that while the office was closed, someone would call once the clinic reopened. He also informed Lacey and Betty of his plans.

He poured a bowl of cereal and dipped his spoon for his first bite when his cell phone rang. He answered it without looking at the screen. "Hello?"

"Elijah?" A familiar, soft, feminine voice greeted him tentatively.

"Mary," he said softly.

Chapter Sixteen

"Mary."

She sighed, loving the sound of his voice, loving... She bit her lip. "How did you make out last night?" she asked.

"My power went out and didn't come on until a little while ago," he admitted. "I woke up freezing and slept by my fireplace." He paused. "How about you?"

"It was too cold upstairs because of the wind, so we stayed by the woodstove in our great room." She smiled. "Even my grandparents. If the wind doesn't die down, we'll all be sleeping there again tonight."

"Let's hope it lets up," he said. "Listen, Mary, I was going to call you today. I've closed the office until Monday morning. Even if the storm passes, the roads won't be passable until they're plowed. Then, if the temperature doesn't rise, it still won't be safe to drive because of ice."

"I figured as much. Thanks for letting me know. No one wants to leave the house in this weather." Then there was silence between them. She was disappointed that she wouldn't get to see him until then. And she almost told him that.

"You have enough food for a few days?" he asked.

"Oh, yes, we have a basement filled with garden vegetable and fruit we canned." She was glad he stayed on the line. "We'll be fine. And there is still plenty of meat in the freezer."

"Good, I'm glad." His voice was soft, sincere. "You have enough charging power for your phone?"

"I charged all of the battery packs for my family in the office this week," she said, "and we haven't needed them yet."

"Wonderful. This way, I'll be able to call again." His words gave her a rush of pleasure, although she knew it was wrong to feel that way about her English boss. She didn't like the thought of not seeing Elijah until Monday, but she knew it was best to have time apart because she had fallen in love with him—an Englisher, who was used to a different way of life.

"Elijah, I… I miss you…working with you in the office, I mean." She might have confessed too much.

He was quiet a moment. "I miss you, too, Mary," he admitted, delighting her. "We'll keep in touch by phone until we can see each other…in the office again?"

Something in his tone encouraged her. "Have a great day. I hope your electricity stays on for you." Mary liked living in her Amish community, but she still longed to have Elijah in her life permanently. Could she switch her way of life? She didn't think so but maybe she'd change her mind.

They said goodbye to each other and hung up. After she closed her flip phone, Mary realized that she hadn't reminded him about his visit for a meal on Wednesday. She hoped Elijah hadn't changed his mind about coming.

As Mary slid her phone into her apron pocket, Mam entered the kitchen. "*Dochter*, we might as well use this time to do our baking."

"Better than doing nothing," Mary agreed. She knew they could clean, but that wouldn't take long since they made a habit of dusting and sweeping each morning after they got up. "Where are *Grossdaddi* and *Grossmammi*?"

"They're napping in their bedroom," her mother told her.

"What about Dat and Simeon?" Mary asked.

"Gone to the barn to care for our animals." Her mother looked concerned. "I suggested they tie a rope to the house somewhere and carry the other end with them so they can find their way back through the blizzard."

Mary frowned and went to look out the side window next to the door that faced the outbuilding. She couldn't see the barn. The wind whipped against the house, rattling the window panes and throwing thick snow, hampering visibility. "No sign of them yet. When did they go out?"

"About forty-five minutes ago," her *mam* said. "It takes time to carry water and fork hay for them."

Narrowing her gaze, Mary searched for the rope her mother told her about. When she couldn't see it, she opened the door, and the wind burst in, bringing into the house frigid air and swirling heavy snow. She quickly closed it after she found what she was searching for. "The rope is tied to the railing. I'll feel better once they step through this door. But I trust Dat, so maybe we should give them a few more minutes before we start to worry."

"I'll make coffee," Mam said and immediately went to work.

Mary stared at the baking ingredients on the counter. "What shall we make first?"

"Muffins," her mother piped up. "Your *dat* and *bruder* love them, especially ones with chocolate chips."

So, Mary went to work mixing muffin batter before adding chocolate chips. Afterward, she filled the tin cups about two-thirds full of the mixture. There was a heavy stomping outside the door as Mary slid the pan into the preheated oven. The door opened, and her father and brother entered the house. She took one look at their red cheeks and snow-covered garments and hats. "You look like snowmen!" she said with a laugh. Then, studying them, she sobered. "You *oll recht*? It's brutal out there."

"We wouldn't have made it back if not for that rope your *mudder* suggested," her father said. He tugged off his hat and gloves and handed them to his wife before he unbuttoned his coat with red hands.

"Simeon?" Mary hurried to help her brother, whose cheeks were pink from the wind and blowing snow. She accepted his hat and gloves, hung them on a hook and then started helping him undo his coat. "Coffee or hot chocolate?" she asked him.

Simeon smiled. "Hot chocolate, please."

"I'll have coffee, Joanna," Dat told her mother.

Mary heated milk in a large saucepan to make hot chocolate and then added unsweetened cocoa powder, sugar and two teaspoons of vanilla. She stirred until it was mixed thoroughly and then ladled out a hot mugful for her brother and herself. The oven timer rang and she pulled out the muffins. The scent of the baked goods merged with the delicious aroma of the hot chocolate, filling the kitchen with yummy goodness.

"Smells wonderful!" Simeon said from the table where he sipped from his mug. "I bet it tastes better."

Mary smiled as she handed her brother a plate with two muffins. "Anyone want to see if our *grosseldre* want to join us?"

"I'll do it," Simeon offered. He was back in less than a minute. "They're sleeping."

Mam nodded. "Let them. I'm just grateful that they're here with us. My *dat* can be stubborn, and I was afraid that he'd refuse to come even though I told him he had to." She handed Dat a cup of coffee. "I'll put aside a few muffins for them, and if they want hot chocolate when they wake up, we can always make more."

The family sat down to enjoy their drinks and muffins. "Everything *okey* with our animals?" her mother asked.

Her father nodded. "Horses have been fed and have water. We made sure we covered each one with a blanket. Our cow seems fine in the back room where the wall is airtight. Made sure she had food and water, too."

"I hope the weather eases soon," Mary said with feeling. "It's not safe to go back and forth to the barn in the storm."

Simeon agreed. "I haven't heard any English vehicles on the road. For sure and for certain, there are no buggies or wagons out and about either. Judging from the amount of snow we're getting, no one will dare to travel anywhere for quite some time."

After he finished his coffee and snack, her *dat* stood. "I'd better bring more wood up from the basement."

"I'll help," Simeon said as he rose to his feet. "Mam, Mary, thanks for the warm-up and muffins."

Mary smiled. "You're *willkomm, bruder.*" She stood and began to gather the dishes to be washed, dried and put away.

While the men headed downstairs, Mary and her mother cleaned up the table and then pulled out more ingredients for baking. They still had a long day ahead of them. No sense spending it being idle. They could make bread, cakes and snack bars. Something to cheer them up and keep everyone's hunger satisfied.

The snowstorm stopped two days after it started. By early Friday evening, Mary heard snowplow engines with the scrape of metal blades, pushing snow off the street. The sound of the plows continued through the night, and with the wind ceasing, the house managed to stay warm in the rooms on the second floor.

Mary talked with Elijah once a day. She was eager to be back in the office, answering calls, checking in patients and doing what she could to ensure the clinic ran smoothly. And where she could spend time with him.

Saturday morning Mary and her family looked forward to eating an early breakfast with her brother David and her sister-in-law Fannie at Fannie's restaurant before the place opened for customers. The eatery was close enough for them to walk, and Mary was glad. After her accident, she was still reluctant to ride in a buggy on a snowy road, although it had been plowed last night. Mary was happy to go because it had been a while since she'd seen her brother and sister-in-law. The storm had kept everyone isolated in their houses, and until today Fannie's place had been closed like the clinic and other area businesses. Mary had a feeling that once the restaurant officially opened, Fannie would be swamped with people keen to get out and enjoy a good meal.

Everyone in Mary's family, except her grandparents who would stay at home, bundled up against the cold before they left. They'd promised to bring home food for Mam's parents. Mary felt warm enough as she walked with her relatives to Fannie's and entered through the rear entrance.

"Mary!" Fannie exclaimed. She smiled. "Mam. Dat… Simeon! It's so *gut* to see you."

"Thanks for having us," Mary said, standing with Fannie while the other members of her family sat in the dining room at a table large enough to hold all the Troyers. "What can I do to help?"

"I've got it," Fannie said.

Mary shook her head. "I want to help," she insisted.

Her sister-in-law grinned at her. "Come with me. You can help take the food out."

Mary picked up a platter of crispy bacon covered with aluminum foil. "Is anyone coming in to help you when you open?"

"Linda is going to try to come in," Fannie said, referring to one of her full-time employees, as she pulled a pan of breakfast casserole from the oven and set it on the counter on a hot mat. "But if she can't make it, I'll manage. I always do."

Mary touched her shoulder. "Fannie, if she can't come in, I'll stay and help you. Better yet, call her to tell her it's *okey* to stay home. That I'll be here to work today."

"I'll do that." Her sister-in-law met her gaze with a grin. "*Danki, schweschter.*"

Mary loved being called *sister* by her brother's wife. "I'll take this out and come right back."

When she returned to the kitchen, Mary gazed with wide eyes at all the breakfast foods prepared by her sister-in-law. "Fannie, do you mind if we send food home with Mam for my *grosseldre*?"

"Not at all," Fannie said with a smile. "I'll pull out some to-go boxes we can fill after we've eaten."

Once the road had been plowed, Elijah decided to head to the clinic to make sure everything was all right. If the place had lost power like at his house, there was a chance that a pipe might have frozen and broken when the temperature inside dropped. Yesterday afternoon, he'd made a call to have the parking lot plowed. He was pleased to see it had been done when he pulled in and parked near the back entrance.

When he walked inside the building, he was glad the lights worked but still worried about water damage. He checked all the areas where there was access to water…and was relieved to see everything was as it should be.

He hadn't eaten breakfast. Suddenly hungry, he decided to see if the eatery Mary had recommended a little while ago, Fannie's restaurant, was open. Her baked goods and breakfast casseroles over the past few weeks had reminded him of the treats he'd loved as a child, and her Amish cooking had been sorely missed over the past couple days while he'd been cooped up at home.

He parked his car next to the place, glad to see vehicles in the lot, and then he entered the building through the front door.

A young Amish woman, wearing a white *kapp* and a patchwork apron over her blue dress, entered from a back room carrying a platter of food in each hand. "Please seat yourself," she said with a smile when she spied him.

Elijah returned her smile and watched as she delivered a meal to a man sitting alone at a table near a side window, then another to a woman across the room. He grabbed a table at the back of the dining room.

"If you haven't seen it, there is a menu in the rack on the table near the wall. Please take your time going over it. Someone will be by to take your order." The Amish server was blonde like Mary, but she didn't look anything like his employee…and friend.

"Fannie," the woman dining alone called. "May I have more coffee?"

"Coming up, Millie!" She stopped at another table. "More tea, Harriet?"

The customer shook her head and asked for the check, and the woman named Fannie promised to bring it to her. He liked the feel of this place—like everyone knew each other. From his experience being raised Amish, the whole community often did.

Another server came out from the back, carrying a coffeepot. She immediately went to Martha's table. "Here you go," a familiar voice said.

Looking over the menu, Elijah caught sight of Mary out of the corner of his eye. He watched as she poured the coffee.

When she was done, she turned to head back to the kitchen and appeared startled when she saw him. Her face turned pale and then reddened. And he frowned.

He quickly smoothed out his expression as she approached his table. "Elijah." She saw his upturned coffee mug. "Coffee?"

He nodded without a word. He'd had no idea that Mary worked two jobs. He thought he'd paid her enough but maybe he was wrong. She poured his coffee and stepped back. "Do you know what you'd like to order?" she asked, looking uncomfortable.

"What do you recommend?" Elijah studied her face, noting the pink that lingered in her cheeks. She was beautiful.

"Everything Fannie makes is wonderful," she told him. "You can't go wrong with any item on the menu."

"Pancakes," he said, "with syrup and bacon on the side."

She nodded and spun to leave. He reached for her hand, and she froze before she turned to meet his gaze.

"I didn't know you worked here." It wasn't his intention to make her uncomfortable.

"I don't," she explained. "I'm just helping my sister-in-law because none of her employees could make it in today."

So, she didn't need the extra cash? He'd promised her a raise and had kept his word. Salaries and wages were direct-deposited every other week. He hoped she would speak to him if she ever felt the pay wasn't enough.

Mary laughed, likely catching the expression on his face. "I'm helping Fannie out, is all. The restaurant is only open for breakfast on Saturdays." She glanced at the dining room wall clock. "We have only an hour left before closing."

Elijah nodded, aiming to sound casual as he asked, "How did you get here?"

She blushed. "I walked with my family earlier. We had

breakfast, and then they left when they were done. I told Fannie I'd stay to help until closing."

He frowned. "Are you going to walk home?"

She shrugged. "I planned on it."

Shaking his head, Elijah said, "I'll drive you home when you're done."

"Elijah…"

"Will you let me take you home, Mary?" he pleaded softly. He needed to know that she'd be okay. The least he could do was get her home safely.

"Okay," she whispered. "We close at eleven today."

"Mary?" Fannie peeked out from the kitchen.

"Coming!" She flashed Elijah a smile. "Pancakes with syrup and a side of bacon," she said. "Anything else?"

He shook his head. "That will be plenty. Thank you."

Elijah continued to watch Mary work the room while he enjoyed his late breakfast. The pancakes were light and delicious. She'd brought him a pitcher of warmed maple syrup, which he poured liberally over the tall stack of hotcakes. The bacon was crispy, just the way he liked it. All in all, he had a wonderful meal and enjoyed every bite. Soon, the other customers left and Elijah paid his bill. Then he sat waiting for Mary, who entered the dining room fifteen minutes later with her coat over her arm.

"We can go out the back," she said.

He nodded and followed where she led. Fannie peered out from inside the kitchen. "Thanks again, *schweschter.*"

She beamed at her sister-in-law. "You're more than *willkomm*, Fannie."

Fannie turned her gaze on Elijah. "You're Mary's boss at Zook Veterinary Clinic."

"Elijah Zook," he introduced himself.

She continued studying him without expression, but then

she suddenly smiled with approval. "You brought Mary her power pack on Thanksgiving. That was kind of you."

He shrugged. "It was a long weekend, and I didn't want her without a cell phone for emergencies."

Fannie nodded. "It's nice to see you again." She turned to Mary. "I'll see you at service tomorrow."

The comment about church reminded Elijah about the differences in his life and Mary's. He swallowed hard but didn't say a word as he led Mary to his car and drove her home. It was only as she opened the car door to get out that he spoke. "Stay warm, Mary." Despite knowing a future with her was hopeless, he couldn't pull his gaze away.

"I'll come for you at the usual time on Monday," he said. He wanted to walk her to the door but decided it was better if he didn't.

She got out and started for the house but then came to his side of the car and rapped on his window. Elijah rolled it down. "Yes?"

"You're still coming to dinner on Wednesday, aren't you?" she asked, worry furrowing her brow.

He knew he should say no, but he couldn't do it. Because any time in her company was well worth the impending heartbreak that would come after it became clear that there could never be a deeper relationship between them, other than friendship.

"I'll be here," he said softly. Besides, he'd already accepted the invitation from her family. He couldn't back out now.

When her gaze brightened, he smiled, then watched as she waved before entering the house. Then he drove home, wondering what he was going to do about Mary Troyer, the woman he cared about more than he should.

Chapter Seventeen

Running into Elijah over the weekend had stirred up new feelings in Mary. She rarely saw her boss outside of work, but she'd enjoyed seeing him in Fannie's, so relaxed as he enjoyed his meal. She'd been touched by his concern and the offer of a ride home on Saturday, and she was eager for the workday Monday, which arrived soon enough.

"Are you glad to be back in the office?" Elijah asked as he hung up his jacket when they arrived at the clinic.

His masculine scent teased her nose, and she inhaled again to fully enjoy it. "I am. It's been a long four days." She set her box of baked goods on a shelf and took off her coat. "I didn't expect to see you at Fannie's on Saturday." She slipped her woolen garment on a hanger.

"I was hungry, and you said the food was good there, so I thought I'd give it a try." He glanced at her briefly. "I was surprised to see you working."

She chuckled. "I'm sure. But Fannie needed my help, so I was happy to stay."

"If you hadn't, I wouldn't have seen you then." His smile and warm tone made her heart start to beat faster.

"And I wouldn't have seen you," she said, smiling inside, pleased.

"I guess some things happen for a reason," he murmured. His blue eyes twinkled as they stepped out into the main room.

"I guess so," she replied before she headed to her desk.

It was hectic from the start, with only minutes to spare to grab something to eat from the break room. By the time the workday ended, Mary was too tired to talk on the way home. He must be exhausted, too, since he hadn't said a word or glanced her way until he'd parked at her door and turned to her.

"Good night, Elijah." She yawned.

He nodded as he yawned in response to hers. "Contagious," he said and then smiled. "We had a tiring but productive day."

Mary nodded. "We did."

"I told Betty she could start this Thursday," he replied, then yawned again. The woman had come in and completed all her orientation paperwork today. Mary liked her already.

"Are you too tired to drive home?" she asked. "I can make you coffee if it will help."

He shook his head. "Thanks, but I'll be fine. Hold on, and I'll get the door for you."

"No need," she said. "No packages or boxes. See?" She held up her gloved hands. "It's only a few feet to the door." She climbed out of his car.

"See you tomorrow, Mary." The crooked smile he sent her made her pulse race.

Mary smiled. "Okay." She then walked into the house and watched his car through the kitchen window until she could no longer see it.

The end of the workday on Wednesday arrived quickly. After last week's cancellations, the clinic had been swamped on Monday and Tuesday, and Elijah was more than ready to leave.

"Elijah," Mary asked, "you're coming for supper, right?"

She didn't have to remind him how he'd promised her father he'd be there. "After I get changed at home." When she gazed at him worriedly, he added, "I promise I'll be right back."

Despite his concern about having a meal with her Amish family, Mary's eagerness for him to be there made it impossible for him to deny her anything. He'd drop her off before heading home to freshen up, and he drove her back to her place with a promise to be back within the hour.

"What are we eating?" he asked as he pulled up to her house.

"I'm not sure. Mam didn't want to tell me this morning what we were having." She shook her head, her eyes filled with affection as she mentioned her mother. He could tell she was excited about tonight. Elijah was too…though he was a little nervous.

"I'm not a picky eater," he said.

She chuckled. "I can attest to that." Mary got out and leaned into the opening. "You better go." She bit her lip. "Hurry back."

The quiet words and her soft smile sent warmth rising up the back of his neck. Inclining her head, Mary stepped back and shut the door. As he drove toward the road, he could see her in his rearview mirror. She stood in the yard, watching him leave. There was no way he wasn't coming back, despite how uneasy he might be during dinner with her family.

After hurrying to clean up and change out of his work clothes, Elijah was back at Mary's house in less than fifteen minutes. He had traded his standard white shirt, black pants and black shoes for a navy sweater over a white shirt and navy corduroy pants with black sneakers. The door opened as he approached the house, revealing the sweet face of the Amish woman he shouldn't think about as often as he did. But how could he not? Mary was beautiful inside and out, always giving of herself with a kindness that was an intrinsic part of her.

She opened the door as he reached her. Elijah lit up inside at her smile. "Am I too late?"

Mary shook her head. "That was quick. You're right on time. Come in." She stepped back.

He'd had second thoughts about dinner with her Amish family. This was the first time he'd had a meal with members of an Amish community since before his family's shunning eighteen years ago. But this was Mary's family, and as he stepped inside, he instantly felt the warmth of the house and the welcoming look her mother gave him. An oil lantern on the table cast a golden glow over the room, reawakening his pleasant childhood memories.

"It's *gut* to see you, Elijah," Joanna said when she saw him. "We're happy you were able to join us."

He smiled. "Thanks for having me." The kitchen table was set with five place settings, letting him know he was the only guest tonight. "It smells wonderful in here. Mary said she didn't know what we were having."

Joanna grinned. "A traditional Amish dish."

He inhaled the food aroma, trying to guess. "Do I detect bacon?" He studied her face.

Mary's mother smiled. "You do."

"Beef pot roast," Mary exclaimed with a grin as she came into the room.

"Is it?" Elijah asked her mother.

The woman nodded. "With sweet-and-sour chowchow and buttermilk biscuits."

"Some of my favorites," Mary exclaimed. She turned to Elijah. "Have you had any of these dishes before?"

He gazed at her with good humor. "Not the way your mother makes them, I'm sure."

"*Dochter*," Joanna told her daughter. "Let your *dat* and *bruder* know that Elijah is here and supper is about done."

"Is there anything I can do to help?" Elijah asked Joanna after Mary had left.

She shook her head. "It's all done, but *danki*. It's nice to know you are a man who is willing to help in the kitchen."

"I have no sisters and always enjoyed watching my mother cook." He had learned a lot from her but rarely had the time to put his cooking skills to good use. His mother didn't make the recipes he'd enjoyed during his childhood, as if doing so reminded her too much of what she'd lost.

Samuel Troyer entered the kitchen. "Elijah! Nice to see you. We are pleased to have you."

Elijah smiled. "Thanks for inviting me. Everything smells wonderful."

Mary returned with her younger brother and immediately locked gazes with Elijah. "Beef pot roast!" Simeon exclaimed. "Yum!"

"Elijah, you sit at the end there, next to Mary's chair," Joanna instructed.

Samuel, Simeon and he sat down. Elijah watched Mary help her mother carry dishes to the table. When all the food was out, Mary and her mother took their seats. Joanna sat next to her husband. Elijah was pleased Mary was beside him.

"Let's bow our heads and give thanks," Samuel said.

Elijah bent his head with his eyes closed and his hands in his lap.

"Father, thank You for the food You have provided for us and for everyone seated at this table, especially Elijah, who we are pleased to have with us this day."

Samuel's words made Elijah feel warm and accepted as more than just a guest.

Mary's father then continued the prayer with thanks for the current good weather. Then Samuel expressed gratitude to Elijah for his helping Mary after her accident. "And we ask an extra special blessing, Lord, for Elijah and his brother Jacob. Amen."

"Amen," everyone repeated.

Elijah hid his discomfort over the end of the prayers, because it reminded him of how it was when he was an Amish child. But then the room became noisy as food was passed around the table, and there was so much for him to keep track of...the meal and the conversation with laughter interspersed that made him smile. Samuel picked up the platter of pot roast and handed it to Elijah, who helped himself before giving it to Mary. He found himself laughing when Simeon commandeered the basket of biscuits as he thanked his mother for making all of them just for him.

With their plates filled, Elijah had his first taste of Joanna's Amish pot roast cooked with bacon. Several spices that he couldn't name burst deliciously on his tongue, and he hummed in appreciation.

Mary stopped mid-fork of chowchow to stare at him and grinned when he closed his eyes after he ate another bite. "*Gut, ja?*"

"Wonderfully outstanding," he said.

Joanna chuckled. "I'm glad you're enjoying it."

He nodded as he forked up a piece of potato roasted with the meat, tasty with the flavor of the beef it had been cooked with.

"So, tell me, Elijah," her father said, drawing his attention. "Zook is a familiar name to us. Do you know where your ancestors are from?"

Elijah stiffened but then made himself relax. "Somewhere in Europe, I think," he said, although the question made him nervous. Mary and her family knew nothing of his Amish early childhood. "I'm guessing from either Germany or Switzerland."

Mary's father nodded. "There are Zooks in Lancaster County. I know of one such family in Happiness. It's a *gut* Amish name."

"But he's not Amish, *Vadder*," Mary said in *Deitsch*.

Elijah didn't react, although he knew what she'd said. "May I have a biscuit?" he asked Simeon, who grinned as he handed him the basket.

The awkward moment passed, and Elijah spread butter on the warm biscuit. Simeon started talking about Snowflake's last visit to the vet. "He's finally eating, thanks to Elijah," he said. The teenager went on so profusely about how wonderful Elijah was that Elijah was relieved when the topic of conversation switched from his background as a veterinarian to a discussion about when winter would finally leave and spring would arrive with warmer temperatures, blooming flowers and the time for planting vegetable gardens.

When everyone was done with the meal, Mary began gathering dirty dishes while her mother wrapped leftovers to store in the refrigerator.

Samuel patted his stomach as he leaned back in his chair. "Mary said you were extremely busy this week," he commented, glancing at Elijah.

"Yes, I'm happy we got caught up after Thursday and Friday's cancellations." He smiled. "Which was why we were able to leave early."

Mary's father nodded. "Simeon, you should show Elijah how well Snowflake's doing. He's filled out nicely. The wet food you provided has been a good start."

"That's wonderful," Elijah said with satisfaction. "I'd love to see Snowflake."

"Why don't you show him now, *soohn*," Joanna said, "while we make coffee and get dessert ready."

"Would you mind?" Simeon asked.

"Not at all." Elijah pushed back his chair and followed Mary's brother. Snowflake was curled up on a pillow that lined his new wooden bed.

Elijah bent down and smiled, stroking a finger along the little dog's fur. "He looks good, Simeon. Healthy. You're doing a fine job with him."

Simeon looked relieved. "Is there anything else I should do for him?"

"The only thing you need to remember," Elijah told him, "is to give him a small portion of his old food whenever you're trying him on new food so he doesn't get sick to his stomach."

"So I should add some chicken and rice to his dry puppy food?" the teenager said, and Elijah nodded.

"Simeon! Elijah!" Joanna called. "Coffee and dessert are ready!"

Mary entered the great room with a smile for Elijah as he stood and met her gaze. "We're having cherry crumb pie," she whispered. "I hope you like it."

"I'm sure I will," he said as he followed her from the room while Simeon trailed behind.

The cherry dessert was scrumptious, and Mary's father convinced Elijah to have a second slice. Elijah lingered for a time until he realized that it was getting late.

"I should go," Elijah said after he finished the last swallow of his second cup of coffee. "Thank you for the good company and the wonderful meal."

"You are most *willkomm*. We're glad you could join us," Joanna said. "Please don't be a stranger. Visit us again anytime."

"That's very kind of you." He stood and looked around at each member of Mary's family. His family would have been like hers, living the farm life and enjoying nightly family meals together, if life hadn't changed so drastically for them.

"Please don't leave yet. I have something for you to take home," Joanna said. She entered another room and returned with a foiled and plastic-wrapped loaf. "It's bread. I just took it out of the freezer, but it will be fine once it thaws." She gave it to him with a jar of red preserves and another bag. "Biscuits," she said. "And strawberry jam for both."

"Thank you," he said, pleased. Her kindness made him warm inside.

When he turned, Mary was there with his coat. She handed it to him in silence and stepped back. "*Danki*, Mary," he said in Pennsylvania *Deitsch* without thinking. But then he froze as he realized what he'd said. Elijah forced a smile at her before eyeing her family. "Thanks again." He addressed Mary alone as he said, "Walk me outside?"

She looked surprised but nodded.

Elijah exited the house and waited for Mary. "I'll pick you up tomorrow," he told her. "Unless you'd rather drive yourself." He liked having her ride with him and hoped she'd continue for a time.

"I'm happy to ride with you." Mary studied him thoughtfully and he knew she had heard his slip into *Deitsch* again.

"Good." He saw her shiver. "You should go inside. It's getting colder." He smiled. "Go on. Don't wait for me to leave. I'll be fine." He climbed into his car, watching Mary enter the house after a quick look in his direction. He waved to her at the door, then put his vehicle into Drive. He headed home with thoughts of the Troyer family…and how comfortable he'd felt during the time spent with them.

Chapter Eighteen

The day started well in the office after she and Elijah had arrived. Lacey was in early, and Betty was ready for her first day on the job.

Elijah appeared at her desk. "Mary, I just got a phone call from Mrs. Weston about her cat. She said she needs to cancel her appointment this afternoon, but neither Lacey nor I can find one for her," he said briskly.

Without another word, he left. Mary wondered what was wrong. He'd been quiet during the drive in this morning, and his continued silence concerned her. He seemed to enjoy last night's supper with her family. What had changed since he left her house? Maybe he just needed cheering up, and his attitude had nothing to do with her.

After checking the schedule, Mary called Mrs. Weston and explained to the elderly woman that her appointment wasn't today; it was for tomorrow afternoon at one. Mrs. Weston promised to come with her cat the next day.

Then she remembered that Simeon had promised to run an errand for her today, and she brightened. Her brother was out cutting pine boughs and holly to decorate the office for Christmas. Surely, her surprise to spruce up the place for the holidays would help lighten Elijah's mood. She called Simeon to ask another favor. "*Bruder*," she said when he answered. "Would you stop by Fannie's on your way and buy four chicken salad sandwiches? I'll pay you when you get here."

"Sure," he said good-naturedly. "Cut greenery and buy lunch for four. Anything else?"

Mary laughed. "Buy yourself lunch, too—my treat—but the Christmas greens and sandwiches are all I need."

"I'll be there in about an hour," he promised.

The waiting room was empty when Simeon arrived with the food and an armful of greenery. "Your sandwiches," he announced as he handed them to her. "Fannie added potato chips." He then lifted the greenery he held. "And here's your first bundle of pine boughs. I have two more outside that I mixed with holly. I'll get them for you."

Mary smiled. *"Danki, bruder."*

"Here you go. Anything else, *schweschter*?" he asked mockingly as he delivered the rest of the greens.

She knew he loved to tease her. "Did you get a sandwich?" she asked. He nodded. "Then you may go now," she replied. "Wait!" she called out when he turned to leave. "Did you pay Fannie for the food?"

Her brother shook his head. *"Nay,* she said it wasn't necessary."

Mary sighed. "I'll take care of it. Thanks again." She'd stop by the restaurant to pay her sister-in-law as soon as she got a chance. Just because she was family was not a good enough reason not to pay.

She put the sandwiches in the refrigerator. Then she went to the exam room where Lacey was assisting Elijah with a patient.

"Hey," Mary said, "there are chicken salad sandwiches in the break room refrigerator with chips."

Then she found Betty near the bath station and told her the same thing. When she was done, she returned to her desk to hide the pine and holly until she was free to decorate. She wanted to do something nice for Elijah and her coworkers.

Mary strung the greens along the top of the windows in the waiting room and lay the intertwined branches across the surface of the reception window. She decided to decorate her area after lunch. Smiling at her handiwork, she breathed in the rich scent of pine that filled the air before she returned to her desk. The only break she took was just before lunchtime when she grabbed chips and a sandwich and ate both standing before she hurried back to work.

A short time later, she heard Elijah, Lacey and Betty talking as they entered the break room to eat lunch.

"Mary, aren't you joining us?" Lacey called out.

Mary peeked into the room, happy to see everyone enjoying the food. "I was hungry and already ate."

"Did you make these?" Betty asked.

Mary shook her head. "My brother brought them. They're from my sister-in-law's restaurant." She caught Elijah looking at her with a somber expression. "Everything all right?" she asked, glancing around the room.

"Fine," Lacey said. "So far, everything is going smoothly."

"Betty?" Mary asked.

"I love working here," Betty replied.

Mary glanced at Elijah again. "Is your sandwich good?"

"Delicious," he replied pleasantly, but he didn't look happy, and Mary had no idea why. Or what was bothering him.

She smiled. "Enjoy your lunch." Then she went to finish putting out the Christmas greenery. The Christmas season should make everyone feel good as it was a special time of year for the Lord, and for friendship and showing appreciation to those around one.

Mary worked quickly to finish her office space before she tucked the remaining pine and holly under Beatrice's desk to be used later in other parts of the clinic, including Elijah's office.

The front door opened, and a couple with a large German shepherd entered the clinic. "Good afternoon," Mary greeted them. "Mr. and Mrs. Rosemont?"

"Yes, I'm Fred Rosemont," the man said, "and this is my wife, Kelly. And this is Rocco. He's here for his first exam. We adopted him two weeks ago. He's a big boy, and we want to make sure he's up-to-date with his shots and medications."

"I'll let Dr. Zook know that you're here," she said as she quickly checked them in. Mary dialed the break room and smiled when Lacey picked up. "Rocco and his parents are here for Rocco's first exam."

"Thanks, Mary," Lacey said. "I'll be right there."

"Lacey will be out to take you to an exam room," she told them as she went out front to pet the German shepherd.

"What a handsome boy!" Lacey exclaimed before she addressed his owners. "Mr. and Mrs. Rosemont? Please follow me. Dr. Zook will be in to examine Rocco shortly." She paused. "I love the Christmas decorations," she whispered, and Mary smiled.

The smile remained on her face as Mary watched Lacey disappear down the hall with their new patient and his parents. She sat back, studying the waiting room and her desk area with satisfaction. All that was needed to complete the holiday look was red ribbon.

It was close to the end of the day when Elijah came out to the front and stared.

"What's all this?" he said in an even voice.

"Decorations. It's almost Christmas." She smiled. "Do you like them?"

Elijah cleared his throat. "Take them all down," he commanded.

Mary blinked. "Why?"

"Decorations are not suitable for this office. Not everyone celebrates Christmas." He clearly didn't like her surprise. "And they are a danger to our patients. Pine is toxic to animals if ingested. And holly isn't much better." He studied the areas she decorated. "Please take them down now," he ordered. Then he spun and left, leaving Mary reeling. She'd never seen him act this way before…not even when they first hadn't gotten along. But then these last weeks, they'd become friends. He'd come to her dinner. Something must be seriously wrong. They'd had a nice time together with her family on Wednesday night, and now here it was the next day and he wasn't the same person.

With tears in her eyes, Mary quickly gathered the greenery and stacked it on the floor by her desk. When she'd collected all of it, she dialed her older brother on her cell phone.

"David? I have some pine and holly here at the office. Can you use them?" When he said yes, Mary sniffed once. "Can you come and get them right now?"

The lump in her throat threatened to choke her as she fought tears. She'd only wanted to make the place nice for everyone.

But all she got for her efforts was her boss telling her to get rid of everything.

Lacey accompanied Rocco with his owners to the front area. Fred Rosemont thanked her and told her he'd call later to make an appointment for their cat, as well. The vet tech was smiling when she headed back inside.

"What happened to the pine and holly?" Lacey asked as if just noticing when she approached Mary's desk. "They looked and smelled so nice."

"Dr. Zook happened," Mary said as she blinked back tears.

The front door opened, revealing her older brother David. "*Schweschter…* You said you have some greens for us?"

Mary nodded. "They're right here. I'll help carry them out for you." She handed David the bundle of pine boughs that she hadn't used yet. Then lifting two other bundles of holly and pine, she took them to her brother's buggy and waited while he stored his in the back.

"Here," she said quietly. "There is one more inside."

David froze and stared at her. "What's wrong?"

"I thought I'd do something nice for the office, but apparently the greens are hazardous to the patients." She forced a smile as she pulled herself together. "*Bruder*, after I get the rest of it, do you think you could take me home? The day is about over anyway. We're not expecting patients."

David looked worried. "Mary…"

"If you can't take me, I can wait, but I'd rather go now."

"*Ja*, of course, I'll take you." He caught her arm as she turned to go back inside. "Do you want me to get the rest of them?"

"It's *oll recht*. I'll get them," she said. "I need to let Elijah know that I'm leaving before I grab my phone and belongings anyway."

David continued to study her. "I'll come inside if you need me."

"I'm fine. I'll be out soon." Mary entered the clinic and gathered the last of the greenery. Lacey came into her area as Mary put on her coat and picked up her belongings. "I need to bring these out to my brother's buggy."

"I can carry them for you," Lacey said, her voice quiet. "You're leaving?"

Mary nodded. "Yes, I need to let Dr. Zook know that I'm leaving with my brother." She shut down her laptop.

"Okay." Lacey followed her outside, and David thanked her as he accepted the last of the evergreens.

Before leaving, she looked for Elijah and found him in his office. "My brother is going to take me home."

He stared at her. "You can't stay?"

"I'm caught up," she told him. "Do you need me to stay?"

Elijah shook his head. "You can head home." He opened his mouth as if to say more but then closed it. "I'll see you again soon."

Unable to respond, Mary could only nod before she left and climbed in next to her brother. She didn't know what was bothering Elijah. Everything had been fine until this morning. Had she or her family done something to upset him? She hoped her parents didn't ask her how Elijah was. Or why she was home early although she did her best to hide that she was upset. They'd become fond of Elijah, and she had, too. But he wasn't the same man who'd come to dinner last evening.

And the realization deeply hurt her.

Chapter Nineteen

"What happened with Mary? Why did you ask her to take down the decorations?" Lacey asked as she entered his office.

Elijah sighed. "I don't like surprises, and we've never decorated for the holidays. Too many chances of our patients getting into them." He regretted the way he'd handled the situation.

Lacey nodded. "I must admit I never thought of that. It's just that Mary was so disappointed. She was trying to do something nice for us."

His heart raced in his chest as he closed his eyes briefly. "I know," he whispered. After spending the evening with Mary and her family, he'd begun to distance himself from her. He realized that they'd made him feel like part of the family, but in reality, he knew she could never be more than his friend, although he yearned for something more.

His assistant's features softened. "You like her." Leave it to Lacey to be direct.

"I can't," he admitted. "She's Amish, and I'm not."

She studied him thoughtfully. "So? That means you can't be friends with her?"

"As I said, it's complicated, and that's all I have to say on the matter." Elijah sighed, feeling exhausted.

"She's a good person. She brings food to share and is always ready to lend a hand," Lacey said. "Why is being friends complicated?"

He stared at her without answering. "It's late. You should go home."

Her expression turned sympathetic. "Fine. I'll leave, but if I were you, I'd fix this, or Mary may never come back."

"I know." He looked away. "I know."

Lacey was silent for a long moment until he met her gaze. "I'm leaving," she said softly. "Have a good night."

"You, too," he said automatically. He was alone in the building. He'd sent Betty home earlier. Elijah hung his head, dropping it into his hands. *What have I done?*

He'd hurt the one woman who meant more to him than anyone. His chest was constricted with pain. Dinner with her family had felt so right...and wonderful. It had given him ideas that he had no business entertaining. The food was delicious, but the company was so much better. And her parents and brother...and Mary had accepted him just as he was.

But they'd be horrified if he'd confessed the truth. Which was why he'd knowingly forced distance between Mary and himself. When he'd picked up Mary this morning, he knew he'd been quieter than usual. If they had chatted, he'd feel hope, and there was no hope in this situation. A shunned man had no business loving a woman of the Amish faith, someone pure and wholesome. And kind and generous.

Still, he had to apologize. He hadn't meant to hurt her. Seeing how she'd decorated the front rooms in the Amish way had brought back memories from his childhood that were still too painful. His family had decorated for Christmas the same way.

Maybe he should tell Mary about his past, as Jacob had suggested. Maybe he was right, and she'd understand. Elijah knew he had to apologize and tell her about his past anyway.

Combing his fingers through his hair, he sat back and debated if this was the right time to tell her. He huffed a breath. No time would ever be right.

After shutting down his computer, Elijah left the building and drove to Mary's house. He was prepared to be treated differently by her family upon his arrival. It had been wrong for him to demand that Mary take down the Christmas decorations she'd been so happy to have put up. For him.

His thoughts on Mary, he didn't realize the sky had darkened since he'd left the office. The first hint of snow fell on his glass windshield, and he turned on his wipers. He didn't care if he got caught in a blizzard. The need to apologize to Mary took priority over his own safety. The snow fell harder, but with no wind, he could still see the road.

His hands tightened on the steering as he caught sight of her house and turned onto the driveway. He parked near the barn and turned off the engine. Elijah remained in his car for several heartbreaking seconds, knowing that what he had to tell her could change everything between them.

But Mary deserved to know the truth. No matter how much it would slay him in the end.

Mary lay on her bed, fighting tears. Why was he pushing her away? She hadn't imagined their growing feelings for each other. Or had she? Maybe she was the only one who felt that way. Once home, she'd gone directly upstairs to her room.

Last evening, Elijah and her family had chatted as old friends while Mary had watched and listened and had become more captivated with the man. So, she was falling for Elijah Zook. So what? He was English, and she was Amish. It wasn't like they could have a life together. She'd contemplated leaving her community before she realized she couldn't abandon her Amish faith. Doing so would be wrong, considering how much *Gott* and her faith centered and guided her whenever she needed the Lord's blessings. Turning to *Gott* once again, she prayed for help in healing from a love that should never have existed. And then she sent up another prayer for Elijah, the man she'd never forget or stop loving...

Mary went to the window, surprised to see snow blanketing the backyard. She took deep, calming breaths and headed downstairs to help her mother.

She didn't know someone had knocked until she saw Elijah Zook standing in the kitchen, chatting with her mother and father. He must have sensed her presence because his gaze found and locked with hers where she stood in the archway between the kitchen and the great room.

"Here she is now," Dat said.

"Mary," Elijah said softly, his blue gaze contrite, mirroring her pain.

"*Dochter*," her mother told her. "Elijah has come to see you. There is something he needs to say."

She looked from Mam to her boss. "Ah...now?"

"Mary," her father said. "Go with him into the other room. Allow him to talk with you."

Mary was shocked to see her *dat* gesturing toward the hallway. She entered the great room, aware that Elijah closely followed her. When her family was out of earshot she asked, "What are you doing here?"

"I've come to apologize," he said softly, "and to confess why seeing your Christmas decorations triggered something dark inside of me."

As she studied him, she couldn't help being curious about what he had to say. She felt a softening for him inside. "Would you want to sit down?" She gestured toward two chairs situated close together, near the first floor bedroom that her grandparents used before they'd moved to the *dawdi haus*.

He inclined his head, his eyes never once leaving hers as he sat down. "Mary—"

"Elijah, you hurt me today. A lot," she told him. "I thought I was doing something nice for you. I'm sorry I didn't ask you first..."

He shifted uncomfortably in his seat. "I'm the one who's sorry," he admitted. "I overreacted, and I want to explain why. Maybe once you hear what I have to say, you'll understand." She heard him inhale sharply. "You may also never want to see me again."

Her heart hurt. "Elijah..."

"Please. I realize this isn't the best time, but I can't allow you to lose sleep over this." His eyes were bright as if fighting tears, which shocked her as nothing else ever could.

The love inside her grew. It might be wrong, but it was something she couldn't control, not since she'd first recognized her developing feelings for him. "*Okey*," she whispered. "I'll listen. Tell me."

His silence made her wait. His features filled with anguish, and she realized whatever he had to say might turn her away from him.

"Elijah." She gazed at him with hope in her heart and a desire to discover the truth about this man.

"Mary, you'll want nothing to do with me once I tell you," he said, his voice quiet.

She shook her head in denial. "Tell me anyway."

His blue eyes glistened. "First, I never meant to hurt you. I reacted badly and took my insecurities out on you."

"I accept your apology," she said. "I should have asked permission before I decorated the office. I was hurt that my surprise wasn't received the way I'd hoped." Moved by his tears, Mary felt a lump in her throat as she blinked back moisture. "But there is more, isn't there?"

Elijah nodded. "We used to decorate our home with greenery such as what you used today. My family, I mean." He stopped and closed his eyes. When he opened them again, the agony in them stole her breath and made her want to hug him tight. But she didn't. Not only was hugging him inappropriate—she needed him to finish.

Mary tilted her head as she studied him. "What does greenery have to do with anything?"

He took a deep breath and then released it. "I grew up Amish, Mary. My family were Old School Amish. Do you know what that means?"

She shook her head, momentarily confused. "Amish?"

"Yes. Have you heard of the Nebraska Amish?" he asked softly, his gaze gentle as he watched her. "Old School is another name for them."

"You were a member of the most conservative and strict sect in Big Valley," she said softly.

He nodded. "Until I was ten."

Something shifted inside as she waited with bated breath for him to go on. "Ten."

"Yes."

"No technology, strict rules," she said. "I remember Dat talking about them once." She paused. "What happened?"

"We were shunned by the church elders," he told her, his voice and expression filled with pain.

"Shunned," Mary echoed. This man was shunned by his Amish community. She thought long and hard about what her father had once talked about at the dinner table.

He was quiet for a moment. "Yes. Forced from our home… we had to start over elsewhere. We sold our farm for next to nothing because only community members are allowed to live there. We loved the Amish way of life, but our church leaders—they were quick to condemn without listening."

Mary drank him up with her gaze. "Your family didn't deserve it," she said, believing it. "You'd done nothing wrong."

Elijah sighed deeply, confirming what she knew without him saying it. "My brother Aaron…he found a cell phone along the road near our general grocery store. He brought it inside to see if he could find the owner. When he couldn't, he walked home and gave it to our parents to hand over to the elders. The next thing we knew, two church elders appeared on our doorstep within minutes, demanding Mam and Dat to step outside the house. Dat sent us to stay in our rooms. When he finally called us downstairs, Dat told us that we'd been shunned and why. Because we had technology—the cell phone. We had to leave our community. At ten, I thought I could explain about the phone to the elders, and they would listen. But they ignored me like I didn't exist." The grief in his voice made her heart hurt for him.

"Elijah, I'm so sorry. That wasn't right or fair." She touched his arm, offering comfort. "That must have been frightening for you," she said, as she slid her hand down to his hand. Mary gave it a gentle squeeze before she let go. "Ten years old?" she asked softly, hurting for the child he'd been.

He nodded. "My brothers and I were all young."

Anger swamped Mary. She had never heard of a child being shunned before. In her Amish community, couples usually join before they marry. Children aren't allowed to belong to the church, until after the age of *rumspringa*, or if they chose to join sooner, even if still single.

Elijah was slumped in the chair with his head in his hands. She pulled away from his clasp to rub the back of his hand with soothing strokes. "Elijah."

He appeared miserable as he looked up.

She softened toward him, wanting only to take away his pain. "I think we should speak to my parents about this."

"I can leave." He avoided her gaze as if unwilling to see the condemnation in her eyes. "They don't have to throw me out."

"It's nothing bad, I promise you," Mary whispered, feeling his sorrow. "But maybe they can help. What happened to you…it wasn't right."

Elijah nodded, then stood and followed her to the kitchen. When he saw both of her parents seated at the table waiting for him, the man Mary loved appeared to withdraw as if eager to leave the house. With a glance at Elijah, a silent message that all would be well, she explained Elijah's story.

"Have a seat," her father invited kindly after he'd listened.

She watched as Elijah pulled the chair out for her, then hesitated a moment before he sat.

"First, your name and the fact that you understood *Deitsch* made me wonder," Dat began. "But it all makes sense now."

"I'm sorry. I know I have no right to be here," Elijah said.

"So your family was shunned when you were but a child." Her father studied him a long moment until the man to whom she'd given her heart inclined his head, confirming it.

"First," Mam spoke up, "your family was treated poorly. The elders should have listened to you and not judged you unfairly. Second, children can't be shunned because they can't be members of the church until they are much older. In our community, betrothed couples join the church right before their wedding."

Elijah blinked several times. "Since it happened, I believed we'd been wronged, but I'd never considered that my brothers and I couldn't be shunned because we were children. Over the years, I mostly shoved it from my mind because it hurt too much to remember."

Mary eyed him with concern. "Your parents should never have been condemned either since they hadn't planned to keep or use the phone but were ready to hand it over to the elders who could have disposed of it for you."

He nodded. "We were forced to leave our home and move to a strange place. I asked my father why we couldn't join another Amish community somewhere else, but he said as shunned members of the Amish faith, we couldn't. So we lived as Englishers after we moved to Lancaster County." He rubbed his right temple. "The small amount of money we made on our farm barely covered the rent for the tiny house we'd found." He closed his eyes. "We were poor. My father had a furniture business in the valley, and all his work had been commissioned by community members. Dat lost his means of support, and it took years to build a business in Lancaster County that could support us. Mam did mending and sewing to earn money. Once we were old enough, my brothers and I took part-time jobs after school so we could help."

"Yes, you and Jacob are successful veterinarians," Mary said.

Elijah smiled. "Jacob and I did well enough in high school and were rewarded with college scholarships. We worked hard and got financial help for vet school after we earned our bachelor's degrees."

"Elijah," Dat said, "you are a *gut* man and don't you think otherwise."

"*Danki*," Elijah murmured, which made Mary smile.

"We'd like you and your family to come for supper," her father said, and her mother agreed with a nod. "If they have trouble accepting our invitation, I'll go over and talk with them."

Mary saw the emotion in Elijah's face. Of hope and gratitude and so much more. He met her gaze, and she saw more than she'd ever hoped for—caring…and wonder and possibly love.

Elijah stood. "I'll ask them."

"Let us know if they resist," her mother said.

He nodded. "I… I don't know what to say, except I have felt comfortable and like part of your family from the first moment I stepped into the house yesterday." Elijah searched her expression. "Will you walk outside with me?"

Mary nodded without looking at her *mam* or her *dat*. "I'll be right back," she told her parents. She followed Elijah to the door.

"Bundle up," he said. "It's snowing."

Mary put on her coat, bonnet and gloves before she stepped outside with him. The snow had tapered to light snowflakes that disappeared as they hit the ground. "A bit different than the night you rescued me," she murmured. When he looked at her, she smiled.

Elijah opened his car door and gestured for her to get in. "Please," he said as if she would deny him. Once inside, he shut the door and got in on the other side. He locked gazes with her. "You believe it? That as children, we're not legitimately shunned."

She nodded. "And your *eldre* should not have been shunned either since they didn't break the rules," she told him. "We can ask Preacher Jonas."

"Mary…what if he doesn't agree?" It was clear to Mary that he had doubts that the preacher would see things the same way as she and her parents.

She frowned. "It doesn't matter, because we believe it. We're friends, Elijah Zook. *Gott* brought us together for a reason. Maybe it's for you and your family to feel peace regarding your past."

He inhaled sharply before releasing his breath. "I hope you're right."

"I am." But she would continue to pray for the Lord's blessing and for the hope of having a future with the man she loved.

Chapter Twenty

"Mom, Dad, why won't you go?" Elijah pleaded when he stopped to see them Saturday morning. "It's just a meal. Mary's family are nice people. What do you have against them?"

"Elijah, they aren't like us," his mother said. "They live differently than we do."

He felt his good humor plummet. He'd had high hopes of convincing his parents to have dinner with Mary's family. And for them to learn they could live in an Amish community again. Elijah had hoped to join Mary's Amish community where he'd have a chance to woo her and perhaps keep her as his own forever. "But we used to enjoy living that way."

"Not anymore, son," Dad said. "That was a lifetime ago."

"Dad, Mom." Jacob spoke up after listening in silence. "I've met Samuel, Mary's father. He is a kind man who accepted my help without issue. If Elijah wants me to go with him, I will." He grinned. "I'm surprised her dad hasn't insisted I visit sooner after I refused to charge them for a veterinary house call."

Elijah glanced at his brother gratefully and mouthed, *Thank you.*

"We can't go," Mom said. "Don't you understand? We're Englishers. They will never accept us!"

"That's not true. They are kind and want to meet you."

Elijah gazed at his father and then his mother. "I love Mary. I love her, and if there is a chance for us to be together, I want to take it. Can't you just have a meal with them this one time?" What would he do if they still refused to meet her family and Mary's father couldn't convince them? Would Mary change her mind about working at the clinic? She'd told him she liked him, and while she hadn't expressed love, the way she'd looked at him made him realize that the feelings between them were real.

His father shook his head. "I'm sorry, son," he said with sadness, but he was firm, and Elijah knew that he'd never change his mind.

He stood, having heard enough. "Thank you for breakfast," he said quietly. Elijah nodded to Jacob. When he looked at Aaron, his brother had a funny look in his expression as if he was struggling to keep his mouth shut.

Elijah put on his coat and hat, then went to his car. The chill in the air made him tug his gloves from his pocket and put them on. He felt a feeling of overwhelming loss and betrayal that his parents hadn't agreed to eat with Mary's family. He drove home. Once inside his house, he went into his living room when a lamp timer had turned on the light earlier. He pulled off his jacket and hat and tossed them onto a chair. Then he sat on the sofa and closed his eyes.

Now he had to tell Mary that except for Jacob, his family had declined her parents' invitation.

"But I will go," Elijah insisted, his voice ringing out in the empty house. "Nothing will stop me from spending time with the Troyers."

Something shut down inside him. He was grateful for his family, the only ones who'd been there for him during the difficult time after they'd left their Amish community.

His eyes stung as he stared at the ceiling. He didn't know

what to do. He knew what he wanted, but would he alienate his parents to have the woman he loved?

Yes. If there was a chance to have Mary in his life. And if there was a chance that she loved him. He would somehow make it work. For to give up Mary was to lose his heart.

After Mary got off the phone with Elijah—he'd called to tell her that his parents wouldn't be accepting their invite—she went to her father. "Elijah's parents declined your invitation, Dat. Elijah asked, and his parents refused. Only Jacob wants to come." A small smile tilted her lips briefly. She was glad that Elijah had his brother's support.

Her father looked thoughtful. "I'll talk to them. What is their address?"

Elijah had told her where his parents lived during their phone conversation, so she gave it to him.

Dat nodded and stood. "I'll call Bert."

Mary smiled. Everyone loved Bert Hadden, the bighearted, tattooed Englisher who gave rides to members of their community whenever they called him.

"*Danki, Vadder,*" she whispered.

"Have faith, *dochter,*" her father said as he awkwardly patted her arm.

As her *dat* planned to visit the Zooks that afternoon, she prayed silently to *Gott* that the Zooks would change their mind. Either way, she needed to confess to Elijah the depth of her feelings for him.

Dat was gone but an hour when Bert brought him home. Her heart began to beat hard as Mary waited for her father to come inside. She tried to read his expression as he entered the house. "*Vadder?*"

He stared at her a moment before he broke into a smile. "Elijah's family will come on the 26th."

"Second Christmas?" she breathed, stunned.

"*Ja*." He took off his coat and hung it on a wall hook.

Mary followed him with her gaze. "They celebrate Christmas then."

"They do. The English way," he said, "but this year they'll join us and be reminded how they once celebrated the Christmas holidays when they were Amish."

"*Danki*, Dat," she whispered.

Her father looked concerned. "Elijah is a *gut* man, but he has lived as an Englisher for many years. He may not be willing to change his ways for you."

Mary fought back tears of happiness. "I know. But it may bring him and his family peace to know that they are not shunned."

"It may," he said, "but it may not bring you the peace and happiness you hope to have with him."

She turned to stare out the kitchen window. "It is up to our Lord, Dat," she replied. "Whatever path *Gott* has chosen for me, I must accept, even if it's not the one I want to travel."

Mary felt the brush of her father's hand on her shoulder briefly before he left her alone to deal with her thoughts.

The side door opened, and Simeon and David burst into the room, both grinning, red-cheeked and carrying an armful of Christmas greens. "Time to decorate," her younger brother announced.

Their good spirits were infectious. "Would you please bring them into the great room?"

Simeon led the way with David slow to trail behind him. "You *gut*?" her older brother asked.

"I'm fine." She flashed him a smile. "How did he get you to help him? You used the greens I gave you, *ja*?"

He nodded. "At the restaurant. I need more for the *haus*. We were looking in the same place so we decided to help each other." There was a twinkle in his blue eyes that spoke of a content life filled with joy. Something she longed for, too. She thought again of Elijah—despite knowing the truth about him now, the obstacles between them still felt impossible. "You love Fannie a lot, don't you?"

David smiled. "I do. She is everything I could ever want in a wife."

"I'm happy for you, *bruder*," she said sincerely. "Come, let's go in before Simeon complains that I am not already there to decorate."

"I'll bring these in but know that Simeon will be coming with me to help bring greenery into my *haus*." David followed her into the great room. After setting the pine boughs and holly where no one could trip on them, he and Simeon left.

Mary assembled a Christmas evergreen spray and tied it with length of red ribbon cut from the spool she'd discovered in the family linen chest. She found pleasure in adding greenery, starting with the great room and then spreading it out to the rest of the house.

And she hoped that this time Elijah would appreciate her efforts…and that his family would, too.

On Visiting Sunday, David, Fannie and Fannie's father and stepmother came for breakfast first thing. After decorating the day before, Mary and her mother had made fresh bread and muffins to go with the eggs, ham and home fries they made, all of which could be warmed up on top of the stove or in the oven.

The morning came and went quickly as everyone enjoyed time spent with family. Midmorning, Fannie's *dat*, Preacher Jonas, and his wife, Alta, left while Fannie and David stayed to enjoy more of the day. At noon, Mam put a premade chicken noodle casserole in the oven to warm before everyone sat down to eat the meal that Mary and her mother had prepared the previous day.

Fannie's homemade carrot cake with cream cheese frosting was put out for dessert. The cake was Mary's favorite, and she felt a little ashamed as she took another piece until everyone else took a second helping, too.

Later in the afternoon, after Fannie and David had left, Mary was upstairs to her room to sew Christmas gifts. Yesterday, she'd baked gifts for the office—four dozen sugar and anise cookies, one dozen of each kind for Lacey and Betty. She smiled as she thought of Elijah and the two batches of rich chocolate fudge she'd made him, one batch with nuts and another without.

She pulled out her sewing project to finish the shirt she was making for him. Mary hoped that Elijah would like the light blue garment as well as the pair of leather gloves she'd bought for him at the store. She wanted him to feel special and treasured this Christmas, especially after learning of the rejection he'd faced as a child.

Tomorrow, she'd work on presents for Elijah's family before they came for Second Christmas, a day reserved for visiting family and neighbors to exchange gifts. Mary knew what she would give them. She hoped that Elijah's family liked the gifts *and* her family.

Chapter Twenty-One

Elijah was nervous as he drove to Mary's with Aaron next to him in his car on December 26. Following them were his parents in Jacob's vehicle.

"What's wrong?" Aaron asked.

Elijah saw concern in his brother's blue gaze. "I don't want the day to go badly," he admitted.

"Mary means a lot to you," Aaron said softly.

Elijah drew a deep breath. "She does and I plan to tell her how I feel."

His brother shifted in his seat. "How would that work—the two of you together?"

"I don't know yet." Elijah turned onto the road where Mary lived. "It depends on whether she'll have me in her life." He paused. "And if her family accepts me."

"They already have, Eli," Aaron said. "Her father visited the house and convinced all of us to come today. His persistence means something, don't you think?"

His eyes on the road, Elijah sensed his brother's smile. "It could mean that Samuel Troyer is a good man who's willing to do whatever it takes to prove that we're not shunned…at least in the eyes of God."

Aaron turned in his seat to face him. "I have no problem with you and Mary."

"Thank you." Elijah met his gaze with gratitude before

his attention was drawn back to the road. He turned onto Mary's driveway and parked in the barnyard. Jacob pulled in and parked beside him.

Elijah got out and reached for the packages on the back seat, handing two to Aaron to carry while he took the rest. Jacob exited his vehicle and opened the door to assist their mother while their father climbed out from the front passenger seat. Turning to his parents, Elijah saw their mother gaze warily at the farmhouse as she waited for her husband to join her. His father carried a gift for Mary's family, and Jacob took from the rear storage area of his SUV a bowl of his mother's fruit salad, her contribution to the meal.

Please let it go well. Please let it go well. The thought reverberated in Elijah's thoughts over and over. As they approached the house, the door opened, revealing Joanna Troyer, Mary's mother, in the doorway with a ready smile on her face for his family.

Elijah sent up a silent prayer to God for his blessings and guidance, and then he asked for the one thing he wanted more than anything. That he and Mary could find a way to be together forever and that everyone in their lives…their families, Mary's Amish community, including her church elders, would accept their love and be happy for them.

"*Hallo!*" Joanna said warmly. "Come in, come in. We're so happy to have you join us." She looked happy as she stepped aside so they could enter. "I'm Joanna Troyer. My daughter Mary works for Elijah."

When Joanna beamed at him, Elijah relaxed. Mary's family were giving people who wanted his family to feel welcome. He was happy to see the wide smiles on his parents' faces.

Elijah stepped up to introduce them. "Joanna, this is my father, James, and my mother, Martha. This is Jacob, the veterinarian who came here to check on Bess, and this is my other brother, Aaron, who owns a furniture shop with my father."

"*Willkomm!*" Joanna said warmly, waving them to come further inside.

"Thanks for having us," his father said sincerely.

"The pleasure is ours." Samuel, Mary's father, grinned at them as he entered the kitchen and saw them. The man's gaze singled him out with an approving look and smile. "Elijah."

"It's good to see you again, Samuel," he said, pleased to feel like a part of the family again.

"The pleasure is mine," Samuel said. "Come in, everyone, and sit down."

"Coffee?" Joanna offered.

"I'll have a cup," his father said.

Jacob spoke up. "I will, too."

And everyone else in his family agreed they'd love to have a cup.

His father handed Joanna his mother's bowl. "It's fruit salad," Mom explained.

Mary's *mam*'s face lit up. "How wonderful! We love fruit salad. Thanks so much for bringing it." There was nothing phony in Joanna's response, and he saw his mother realize it.

"You're welcome," his mom replied, appearing pleased. "I'm glad you like fruit. I wasn't sure what else to bring."

"It wasn't necessary to bring anything but this looks delicious! I'm happy you did." Joanna led his family to the kitchen table. There were no place settings yet, but Elijah saw the stack of dishes, utensils and napkins on the counter, ready to put out.

Coffee was poured for everyone, including Joanna and Samuel. Elijah couldn't help searching for Mary.

"She's upstairs," Joanna told him with a knowing smile.

His mom sniffed appreciatively. "It smells wonderful in here!"

"We're having roast beef, baked potatoes and sides," Joanna said. "I hope you like them."

"Roast beef is one of my favorites," his dad said.

The outside door opened, and Mary's brother Simeon entered the house.

"Simeon, this is my family," Elijah said. "My parents, James and Martha, and my brothers, Jacob and Aaron."

Simeon nodded. "*Gut* to meet you." He looked around the room. "Where's Mary?"

"Right here." Dressed in a green dress with a white cape tucked into a white apron and her lovely blond hair tucked under her white organza *kapp*, Mary entered the kitchen with her beautiful smile. "*Hallo!*" She greeted his parents with the same warmth her mother had given his family.

He saw his parents studying her. "Mary," he said, hoping to draw her attention.

"Elijah," she murmured, and the look in her blue eyes captured his heart just as she did every time she was near him.

"Mom, Dad, this is Mary," he politely introduced them.

Simeon had gone to the window. "Mam? David and Fannie are here."

"Open the door and let them in," Samuel said.

Elijah watched as Mary's brother entered the room with his wife, Fannie, whom he'd met in the restaurant previously. He stood. "David, Elijah Zook." He turned to Fannie. "Great to see you again. Your pancakes were delicious!"

Fannie chuckled. "Come by anytime."

David, however, eyed him as if reserving judgment. Elijah held his gaze, unafraid. Mary whispered something in her older brother's ear before she came to sit beside him. David's expression softened as if he understood now that Elijah and Mary had resolved their differences.

"Desserts," Fannie said as David handed a covered pie plate to Joanna. "Brown sugar cake." Fannie placed a second, much larger container on the kitchen counter. "And whoopie pies," she announced with a smile.

Elijah saw the look on Aaron's face and said he was eager to try one. It had been a long time since any of them had tasted the Amish treat. "Aaron loves whoopie pies," he said with a smile for his brother.

Mary glanced around the table, pleased that everyone seemed relaxed and happy. So far, it was turning out to be a good day. She snuck a glance at Elijah beside her and saw with a rush of pleasure that he was gazing at her with a small smile.

"I understand that you design and make furniture," her father said to Elijah's dad.

"I do," James replied. "It's something I've always enjoyed."

Her *dat* appeared interested. "I might like to commission a piece from you. Can we discuss it later?" James agreed.

"Why don't you men go into the other room, so Mary and I can set the table?" her *mam* suggested.

Elijah stood with the others but looked reluctant to leave her.

"It's *okey*," she murmured. "We can talk more later."

He gave her a nod before he followed their fathers and brothers from the room.

Martha rose from her chair. "What can I do to help?"

"You can relax," her mother said.

"I'd rather help," Elijah's mom said. "Please let me."

Fannie quickly joined in. "Same for me."

"All right." Mam gestured toward the dishes on the counter. "Everything is there for the table." She opened the oven door to check on the roast and potatoes. "Everything is coming along nicely and will be done in about twenty minutes. Fannie, would you please get the dried corn casserole from the refrigerator? It just needs to be warmed."

Fannie nodded and obeyed. Her *mudder* continued, "Martha, what do you and your boys like to drink with your meal? We have coffee, tea, soda and water. Oh, and lemonade, too."

"Any of those will do," Martha said with a chuckle as she put out the last place setting.

"I'll ask them," Mary offered.

"That would *wunderbor, dochter*," Mam said.

When she entered the great room, Mary felt a sudden tension. Her gaze went immediately to Elijah, who looked uncomfortable but didn't avoid her gaze. "Mam wants to know what you all would like to drink?" She listed all the options her mother had mentioned.

Mary noted each of their drink preferences, and then with one last assessing look around the room she left, worried that something might have gone wrong. She returned to the kitchen where the smell of her mother's pot roast hung in the air, offering warmth and comfort. "Is it too early to pour drinks?"

Her mother nodded. "Go ahead, Mary. I'm going to take out the roast and potatoes. And while you're in the refrigerator, would you please take out the yum-yum salad?" The orange-flavored side dish was an Amish dessert with orange-flavored gelatin, canned pineapple, cream cheese, sugar, and mandarin oranges all folded into either thawed cool whip or freshly made whipped cream. Mam had used thawed cool whip for convenience since there had been a lot of dishes to prepare for this meal.

Soon, the women put out the food with the drinks that each person requested. Mary felt her stomach burn as the men filed back into the kitchen. Elijah gave her a reassuring look, and she tried to relax.

"Who would like to say grace?" her mother said.

"I would," Elijah said, much to his family's surprise. "Please bow your heads. Dear Father, our God, thank you for the food before us. Everything smells delicious, and I'm eager for a taste."

Mary smiled when she heard Jacob and Aaron chuckle.

"But most of all," Elijah continued, "I thank You for bringing all of us together… Mary's family and mine. This is a special day, and I'm grateful for Your blessings and goodness, oh, Lord. Amen."

It stayed quiet for a moment, and then everyone started to speak, praising Elijah's grace and the food as dishes were passed around the table. She loved Elijah's prayer, and she loved the man next to her.

The tension she'd felt when she'd entered the great room was absent, and Mary prayed that it would stay away. Glancing about the table, she felt peace and hope for the future.

When the main part of the meal was finished, Mary, her mother, Fannie and Martha cleared the table to make room for the desserts. Mam put on another pot of coffee and filled the kettle for tea for anyone who wanted it.

As everyone ate dessert and relaxed over a second cup of coffee and tea, Mary heard a knock on the door, but before she could get up, her father was already there to answer it.

"Jonas! Alta! Come in," Dat invited. "We weren't sure you could come, but we're glad you did."

"We finished up at our *soohns' haus* early, so we thought we'd stop by," Jonas said as he stepped inside, his gaze going around the table.

"Would you like dessert?" Mary asked.

"*Nay, danki.* We had more than our fill at DJ and Danny's,"

Jonas said and then explained for their guests' benefit, "Our twin sons own a construction company and bought a house together in Bluebell, north of here."

Her *dat* shifted chairs and added two more from the other room. "Have a seat."

Jonas shook his head. "I'm sure Alta wouldn't mind sitting, though." Mam poured Alta a cup of coffee, and the woman smiled her thanks.

"*Hallo*," Jonas greeted Elijah's parents. "I'm Preacher Jonas Miller." He smiled at Elijah's mother and father. "Would the two of you and Elijah be open to talking with me?" He became quiet. "In the great room, if you'd be willing."

James sighed with acceptance, but his wife, Martha, looked uncomfortable and ready to argue.

"Dad, Mom, please," Elijah pleaded. "It's okay. Please come with me into the other room."

Mary felt concern for him. To her relief, Elijah's parents and brothers, as well as Elijah, followed Jonas and her father into the other room. She became sick to her stomach when they were gone for a long time. When they finally came back, Mary studied their faces but couldn't tell what anyone was thinking. Elijah drew her gaze and gave her a nod and a smile, and she grew hopeful that the discussion with Jonas had gone well. She would find out from Elijah—but when they got a chance to speak alone. Now wasn't the right time.

The fact that the Zooks didn't immediately leave was a good sign. It was dark after the light supper Mary's family had served, when his parents thanked her for the meals and a lovely day.

As Elijah's parents and brothers got ready to leave, Mary remembered the gifts she had for all of them. "Wait just a minute, please! There is something I'd like to give you." She ran upstairs and returned with the presents. For his father and brother Aaron, she'd hand-painted the lettering on a wooden sign with 'Zook Furniture Treasures, James and son Aaron, Proprietors.' She'd made his mother a full-length patchwork apron in shades of blue and green. Jacob received a large box of her homemade cinnamon rolls and the small wooden horse she'd bought at Kings to display in his office because of his equine veterinary specialty.

"Please take these gifts," she urged them. "You can open them at home." She smiled as they took the packages. "And thank you for coming. Have a blessed Christmas and a safe trip home."

His family left, but Elijah stayed. "Preacher Jonas, may I speak with you again in the other room?" The elder left the kitchen with Elijah. They were gone a few minutes before they returned. "Alta, my love, are you ready to head home?"

"Always." Alta smiled at her husband as she stood and put on her coat, which Jonas held open for her.

"Thank you for coming," Mary said to the couple.

After they left, Elijah told her he needed to talk with her privately. Mary glanced at her father, who nodded approval.

Elijah gestured for her to sit in the same chairs they'd sat in when he'd confessed his past to her. "Earlier, Jonas asked my parents and brothers questions. Do you know what your preacher said?"

Mary shook her head. If Jonas didn't understand, then Elijah's family would forever be shunned without reason.

"Jonas believes we were treated unfairly by our church elders. It disturbs him to know that men of God exist who misjudge and mistreat their church members without once listening to what they have to say."

The preacher's confirmation said it all and hopefully offered the family some peace. It was what Mary had hoped for Elijah and his family. "I'm glad."

"There is something else I need to tell you," he said, his expression serious. "If it bothers you, just let me know, okay?"

She was suddenly nervous since she had no idea what he wanted to say. "Okay."

"You and I have lived much different lives," he began.

Her eyes stung as she agreed.

He drew a breath before he continued. "Tell if I'm wrong, but I think there is something special between us…something I don't want to let go of."

Hope unfurled inside her. "What is that?"

"Love," Elijah said. "I know we didn't have the best start, but as I got to know you, I realized how special you are. Thoughtful, kind, with the warmest heart I've ever encountered. So, I was wondering if you'd allow me to officially court you. I spoke with Jonas, and he agreed that I could ask you, but that I needed to prove that I can live happily in the Amish community. Now, you don't have to decide this very minute…" He reached for her hand and held it gently. "I know I've acted badly at times, but only because I'd been drawn to you with no hope for a future. I'm sorry. I tried to distance myself from you and became frustrated because I couldn't stay away." He blinked rapidly. "Mary, I promise to be a better man for you."

"It may not be easy for you to live in an Amish community again," Mary warned, her eyes filling. "But I trust you. I've seen the man you are. So, yes, you may court me when the time is right."

"Yes?" he repeated, as if surprised that she was willing to give him a chance.

"Yes, I would like that," she told him. "We can do whatever it takes for us to work through our differences should they arise in the future. But, Elijah, if you haven't figured it out yet, I think you're special, too, and I love you."

"I love you, too," he said, his features filled with joy.

Mary sniffed and blinked back tears. "Praise the Lord."

And Elijah smiled. "Amen."

Epilogue

Two and a half years later

Elijah set down his mug after he finished his coffee. "Mary, are you ready to go?" he called.

"Be right there!" she answered, her sweet voice warming his heart.

Elijah felt a familiar contentment, thinking about all the changes in his life. His parents and two brothers had decided to continue the English way of life but he was thrilled to be Amish again, especially since he and Mary had been allowed to marry.

It had taken Elijah a full year to convince Jonas and the church elders that his return to the Amish faith was what he wanted.

His wife rushed into the room, wearing a light blue tab dress that highlighted the color of her eyes but didn't hide her baby bump. "What time is it?" she asked as she adjusted her white *kapp* by tugging gently on its strings.

"Fifteen minutes past time to leave for work," he said with good humor.

"I'm sorry," she breathed as she rubbed a hand over her swollen belly. "Will Jacob be mad at me?"

He put his arms around her. "Never. You've somehow managed to get him wrapped around your little finger."

"Elijah," she gasped with laughter. "That's not true."

"Wife, soon you'll be giving birth to his niece or nephew," he whispered in her ear as he held her. "You know how much he's looking forward to it." He released her and stepped back after giving her a sweet kiss.

"Let's go." He slipped his arm around her waist, walked her to their buggy and lifted her inside. "We'll be easing back on our hours next week. Jacob doesn't mind. There is someone from his former practice who's looking to join a smaller office."

He and Mary still worked at the clinic, but not for long. Beatrice had returned and then retired a year later to move in with her sister, and a new manager was hired. Over a year ago, after the wedding, Elijah had asked Jacob to leave his practice and partner with him in Zook Veterinary Clinic. And his brother had accepted since his former practice had already hired a new large animal vet. Then Elijah sold Jacob his small house, which was better suited for Englishers and close to the clinic. With money Elijah had gotten for the house and his brother's partnership, Elijah had purchased a larger Amish home down the road from Jacob and their clinic. Besides selling his house to Jacob, he'd given his car to Aaron, who'd been driving an old clunker.

The church elders had permitted Elijah to keep his business because of his service to the community as a local veterinarian. But since learning of Mary's pregnancy, he'd decided to cut back on their work hours until the baby was born when he'd reaccess what he wanted for the future. He liked working as a vet, but he wasn't sure if he wanted to be in the office every day or spend most of his time out in the Amish community making house calls to treat farm animals while Jacob worked in the clinic. Whenever a need arose for an equine vet, Jacob would work in the field while Elijah covered the clinic.

"Elijah?" his wife whispered as they headed to the office in their new family buggy.

"*Ja?*" It'd been easy for him to slip back into Pennsylvania *Deitsch*, the language of his childhood. He felt her hand settle on his shoulder. He looked at her with a frown. "What is it, *Frau*?" he asked with concern. It was too early for their baby's birth. "Are you *oll recht*?"

"*Ja*," she assured him.

"Then tell me what's wrong?" he insisted.

"I can't," she said softly. "Because everything is perfect. I just need to say I love you."

He released a shaky breath before he beamed at her. "And I love you, *meine frau...meine liebe.*"

And they gazed at each other with wide smiles on their faces as they basked in the warmth of the summer sun and the joy of knowing they'd been blessed by *Gott* with their love and the support of their families, their neighbors and their church.

* * * * *

If you enjoyed Her Amish Winter Match
Be sure to catch David and Fannie's story

His Forgotten Amish Love

Available now from Love Inspired.

And discover more at Harlequin.com!

Dear Reader,

Mary Troyer, the Amish heroine, is the sister of David Troyer, who found his true love with Fannie Miller in my book, *His Forgotten Amish Love*. For six months, Mary has worked as the assistant to the office manager of Zook Veterinary Clinic but has had little contact with the grumpy English owner, Dr. Elijah Zook. When the manager takes an extended leave of absence, Mary is forced to work with the man who scowls whenever he sees her. Why doesn't the man like her? His reasons are complicated and have to do with his secret past.

The timeline of Mary and Elijah's story is between *His Forgotten Amish Love* and *A Convenient Christmas Wife*, which features Joshua Miller, a widower, and Esther King in a marriage of convenience and inspirational romance.

I hope you enjoy this tale of an Amish woman and an English veterinarian…and the complications of a friendship between two people with different lifestyles that develops into something more.

May you be blessed with good health and a life filled with joy.

Love and light,
Rebecca Kertz

Get up to 4 Free Books!

We'll send you 2 free books from each series you try
PLUS a free Mystery Gift.

FREE Value Over **$25**

Both the **Love Inspired®** and **Love Inspired® Suspense** series feature compelling novels filled with inspirational romance, faith, forgiveness and hope.

YES! Please send me 2 FREE novels from the Love Inspired or Love Inspired Suspense series and my FREE gift (gift is worth about $10 retail). After receiving them, if I don't wish to receive any more books, I can return the shipping statement marked "cancel." If I don't cancel, I will receive 6 brand-new Love Inspired Larger-Print books or Love Inspired Suspense Larger-Print books every month and be billed just $7.19 each in the U.S. or $7.99 each in Canada. That is a savings of 20% off the cover price. It's quite a bargain! Shipping and handling is just 50¢ per book in the U.S. and $1.25 per book in Canada.* I understand that accepting the 2 free books and gift places me under no obligation to buy anything. I can always return a shipment and cancel at any time by calling the number below. The free books and gift are mine to keep no matter what I decide.

Choose one:
☐ **Love Inspired Larger-Print** (122/322 BPA G36Y)
☐ **Love Inspired Suspense Larger-Print** (107/307 BPA G36Y)
☐ **Or Try Both!** (122/322 & 107/307 BPA G36Z)

Name (please print)

Address _____ Apt. #

City _____ State/Province _____ Zip/Postal Code

Email: Please check this box ☐ if you would like to receive newsletters and promotional emails from Harlequin Enterprises ULC and its affiliates. You can unsubscribe anytime.

Mail to the Harlequin Reader Service:
IN U.S.A.: P.O. Box 1341, Buffalo, NY 14240-8531
IN CANADA: P.O. Box 603, Fort Erie, Ontario L2A 5X3

Want to explore our other series or interested in ebooks? **Visit www.ReaderService.com or call 1-800-873-8635.**

---

*Terms and prices subject to change without notice. Prices do not include sales taxes, which will be charged (if applicable) based on your state or country of residence. Canadian residents will be charged applicable taxes. Offer not valid in Quebec. This offer is limited to one order per household. Books received may not be as shown. Not valid for current subscribers to the Love Inspired or Love Inspired Suspense series. All orders subject to approval. Credit or debit balances in a customer's account(s) may be offset by any other outstanding balance owed by or to the customer. Please allow 4 to 6 weeks for delivery. Offer available while quantities last.

Your Privacy—Your information is being collected by Harlequin Enterprises ULC, operating as Harlequin Reader Service. For a complete summary of the information we collect, how we use this information and to whom it is disclosed, please visit our privacy notice located at https://corporate.harlequin.com/privacy-notice. Notice to California Residents – Under California law, you have specific rights to control and access your data. For more information on these rights and how to exercise them, visit https://corporate.harlequin.com/california-privacy. For additional information for residents of other U.S. states that provide their residents with certain rights with respect to personal data, visit https://corporate.harlequin.com/other-state-residents-privacy-rights/.

LIRLIS25